Daphne's Seasons

Naomi Gal

PublishAmerica
Baltimore

First printing

ISBN: 1-4241-5741-2
PUBLISHED BY PUBLISHAMERICA, LLLP
www.publishamerica.com
Baltimore

Printed in the United States of America

SUMMER

I fell in love with the barn at first sight. We did. How long is it going to take before I stop we-ing? There is only me. Or we in the past tense. Well, I first fell in love with the little farmhouse next door, but you said, "Come on, look at the *real* thing," and I did and you were right, as always.

So yes, we saw the barn together, and we both fell in love with it, we looked at each other, and I caught the impish spark in your dark blue eyes, and I knew you were hooked. I was too, but I played the reasonable. "It is far too expensive," I whispered in your ear when the realtor turned her back to us. I could have said it out loud: chances are her Hebrew wasn't that good. If any.

But at that moment I knew we were going to live here happily forever after.

What I never, ever realized is that I would live here on my own, and that you would be gone to forever after, wherever that is.

Here I am, moving in today, on my own, confused, exhausted, distraught, jet-lagged, the flight was by far too long, I couldn't sleep a wink. I cried, obviously, this is one trip we were supposed to take together. But right now I am too busy getting settled in our—my—barn and my hands are full. The barn looks so much bigger than it did when we first saw it. Maybe because now it is all mine. "It sounds far too big for you," Dea said, "but hopefully it will keep you busy." And busy I will be once the container with our—my—stuff will arrive. All I have right now are the two suitcases I brought with me and some groceries I picked up on my way.

I keep feasting my eyes on the dark brown beams crisscrossing the high, magnificent ceiling, the ladders climbing up the walls, made from the same wood, on both sides of the entrance hall. You can still detect the marks the builders made while matching the beams. Never have I lived in a place as glorious as this barn.

My first dinner in my new kingdom is not as bad as I had anticipated. Sitting at the big window seat in the living room, watching our meadow, and the corn in the fields growing green and tall, getting acquainted with the only neighbors we have, some of them creatures I have never seen before: groundhogs grazing with zeal, every now and then raising their heads to check around. A couple of graceful deer cross the lawn, wagging vigorously their tiny white tails. Raccoons, I haven't met yet, but I guess their presence in the forest surrounding us. Squirrels rushing back and forth in a furry hurry, butterflies expose their beautiful colors, flying like the singing and screaming birds whose names I still have to learn. I will not be alone here, Alon, obviously lonely for you, like I am at the moment, sipping my wine out of a paper cup you would have despised, a concession made when moving into a hardly furnished barn starting from scratch in the middle of one's life.

And you are here; I feel your presence everywhere. You particularly like—not surprising—hanging out in the ghost wing. I opened the door and closed it at once; something is lurking out there, not merely your ghost. Maybe tomorrow I will have more courage to venture into the haunted space. The owners started remodeling it and gave up; most probably they didn't need another wing—the barn is big enough as it is. I wonder if you will be up in my new bed, between the fresh sheets, playing your favorite prank: the dead. Maybe you will spare me your antics in this novel environment.

I gaze out the window and there you are, all over the place, Alon, the Hebrew word for oak. Trying to postpone going to bed, still scared of your absence, I am listening to the sounds. Every house has its own language, a series of sounds no other house has. The barn is creaking every now and then; the wood is old and complaining. The silence outside doesn't frighten me. I soak it in like in a healing potion, after the sound and fury back home. I dread lying awake in bed without you, waking up in the morning not remembering you are gone. But I do crawl in between sheets that have no recollection of you. I fall asleep, the wine, the jetlag, the panic alarm that goes with the forlorn territory—all lull me into a dreamless slumber. I wake up at dawn knowing for the first time that you are not by my side. This is my bed and you never slept in it. I don't need to search for your fading scent on the pillows. I can't help feeling mild relief. Don't be angry, darling. As you can see—can you?—I am still addressing you incessantly. Talking to the dead.

*

You hovered over me all day long, so what else is new, stating constantly, *I would have done it better.* I guess you are right. It is all too strange and new to me, and I was never good at organizing. Or so you said.

I am amazed by the totally unpredictable weather. A promising sun was shining this morning, and all of a sudden the sky got clouded and torrential rain poured down. An hour later the sun was smiling again, the sky clear as if nothing had happened. The green all around caresses my eyes, soothes my lungs, spoils the desert woman in me, so used to the scorching sun, blazing almost all year round. I feel a constant relief; do you think it will fade away with time? It is strange, Alon, isn't it, to feel relief being away from our relentless homeland on one hand and on the other hand to feel so bruised and pained by your horrible, senseless absence.

I am shopping like there is no tomorrow and frankly there is no time; soon I start teaching and I want the barn to be home by then. Incredibly huge malls with everything your heart desires if-you-have-the-means. The mall is America's kingdom and salvation.

I get lost time and again, never remembering where I left the car, roaming parking areas in search of a vehicle I hardly know. I lost my way coming back home, taking unknown roads, turning in circles for hours, too embarrassed to ask for directions, sometimes not seeing a living soul for miles at length. Don't laugh. I bet it would have happened to you as well, although you know the area. But somehow you would have made it look okay. As if that was the shortest way, or the only one possible. Not great at admitting your mistakes. Or ever apologizing. But no posthumous fight with you. Do I sound angry? I am in my anger phase, darling, they say it is the one before reconciliation, acceptance. Will I ever get there? Will I cease asking what you would have said/done? Will you ever leave me, go away, and stop dominating my thoughts? Will I live forever in this engulfing cloud of sadness and loss?

I can't believe the kindness of people here. Lea and Josh drive over to make sure everything is okay, bringing takeout food, installing the bed and putting on the sheets before I arrived, easing my new life in every possible way. Strangers here are so nice and warm, even at stores, it takes me by surprise after the tough people back in our un-holy land. It wasn't always that way. We used to be bright and welcoming, but harsh realty turned us hard.

It is still strange for me to enter any store—and probably restaurants, coffee shops, cinemas and theaters—without having to open my handbag for inspection. I still have the automated reflex of preparing the bag beforehand. It will take awhile to unlearn. You claimed human beings could and would get used to the worst. So say, my precious Alon, how come I cannot get used to your absence?

The grief and loss wait for me everywhere, ready to attack and hurt, remind me of your absence in the cruelest ways. Dark and dismal when I am walking down the aisles of the food store, and without thinking grab something for you and put it in my cart. You are no longer here. You see me; I sometimes buy it rather than put it back on the shelf.

I saw your grimace when I faced the no-established-credit ordeal. So if you are so smart, Alon, how come you did not warn me? You knew we would stumble into this catch-22. As an American you were familiar with the system, right? I am not making a scene, honey, just very tired and upset. Why do I apologize? You are dead and that is why I have to struggle on my own with a whole new and unwelcoming set of rules. Yes, it is the famous anger stage but it beats the previous denial, right? Still, you would have been proud of me when I leased the car—with no established credit, Lea signed for me—and returned the rented one. Four-wheel drive, you would have loved it. I enjoy driving here, and you know how I resented driving back home, where every driver on the road has a contract on you, as you used to say. You were the driver while I sat mute by your side, and when once in a blue moon I was at the wheel you criticized incessantly, was I that bad?

Here I am, without a phone yet, but who needs one when I can communicate with you so freely. The container, supposed to have arrived today, is being held in NY for a random inspection. The movers said I have to pay the bill; otherwise they will not deliver it. Infuriating, but what can I do? Right, I will not send bills to your afterworld, but I can imagine the scene you would have raised. You were short tempered, my darling, you cannot deny it. Still, it would have been easier with you around; at least I would not have felt so isolated. I called Dea from the mall and she sounded guilty for not being here to help. I made light of it but I am not going to lie to you. I never knew I could experience such an overwhelming loneliness. Sitting at my window seat, I wait exhausted for the sun to set after a warm, balmy day.

Come sit with me at my favorite window seat. My tiredness and exasperation fade when I look at the lush meadow and the thick greener-than-green forest all around. The sun is sinking slowly and gracefully, casting a glowing pink and orange haze all around. I can see the reddened creek shining crimson and silver twisting, playing hide and seek among the trees.

Want to take a walk down there with me? Probably not. You would have been immersed in something; writing, reading, gazing at your computer, and I would have gone on my own anyway. Or maybe you would have joined me; there is nothing, yet, in the empty house to keep you busy.

Off we go, Rita and I. Right, you prefer to call her Marguerita, you and your literary names, but it is a long name for a hybrid mixed

Canaanite dog. Rita is still apprehensive, and I don't think it is jetlag. The dog who roamed Jerusalem's streets, unafraid of buses, fumes, crazy drivers, urban hazards, bigger dogs, bombs and terror, is now too scared to leave the barn. She listens puzzled to the forest sounds, flinches when she hears the crickets chirp, runs home wildly when a wasp tries out her fur.

I watch with awe the Great Fireflies Evening Performance. Once the light fades they start dancing around, imitating the stars above, glittering, shimmering, iridescent, dazzled and dazzling, intoxicated with their own light, intoxicating me. Fireworks of sparkling bugs performing their nightly pyrotechnics—a love rite, I am told. Rita jumps around, yelping excitedly, trying to catch one, falling back frustrated. You would have laughed. But then, lots of things would have made you laugh. Starting with my coming here on my own. Proceeding with our plan as if nothing had happened. But most probably you would not have laughed. You would have been angry. You would have felt as if everything goes on without you. And it does, my love, it certainly does. Death was never part of your plans, nor mine. You always acted so immortal.

Your brutally stupid superfluous death. You know I have thought about it endlessly. Is death—any death—superfluous? Especially your kind of death? I am not even sure I can call it "political" death since it didn't serve any purpose. Or it did, the purpose of the terrorist who took you and the others? Would you have minded that she was a woman? I don't know. Sometimes I think you might have seen her and understood what was going on before the light faded on you forever, or maybe you never knew what hit you, as many people bothered to assure me.

I am not going to think about it. My surroundings are too beautiful. I should never ever take them for granted. The serenity is a study in contrast. I don't want to poison it all with my nightmarish memories. But maybe they enable me to appreciate it to such an extent. Still, we both appreciated it when we came to sign your contract and found this haven. We were exhilarated. I felt as if we were having a second honeymoon. Certainly the last.

Remember they were plowing the fields around the barn? Look at them now. The corn is growing verdant and tall, thriving up toward sky and sun.

So you never came here as the Great Writer in Residence. And I am here, the Widow-Editor-Assistant of the Would-Be Writer in Residence. Unbelievable, isn't it? But then the whole thing is, and I can hear your voice saying, "The unbelievable is our daily routine." Do I misquote you? I am entitled, you know, there is no one to tell me off.

I am not sure if my new career would have made you laugh. I am afraid you would have been furious because I dare step into your big shoes and teach some of your classes. But you know it wasn't my idea. Professor Bernard called and offered me a job three weeks after your death. I was out of words and he said, "Maybe it is too early, but I want you to think about it and I will call back."

Dea said at once, "Grab it! It is the best remedy." Coming from our psychologist daughter, who could argue? But I did. I had so many considerations, inexperience, language difficulties, relocating on my own, mainly the fear of not being able to deliver, nothing like what you were going to give the students. I know I am not even second best. How can one compare to you?

Sometimes I feel you know it all. As if you are watching from up there or down or wherever you are. Your voice speaks in my mind. Most of the time it criticizes me. The way you did when you were still breathing down my neck. Maybe I am being unjust but you can't defend yourself, can you?

*

The telephone was installed. I can renew my contacts with the world, although I am getting accustomed to the incredible silence, imbibing it with every pore like rich nectar. I take Rita out twice a day. She won't go on her own. The forest's fresh smells puzzle her and the sounds are too frightening. We take long walks and she has to bear with me while I gorge on our raspberries growing along the long dirt road leading to the barn. There are signs stating *Private road! No trespassing! No hunting!* And although it spells isolation I marvel at my newfound serenity.

I smelled a rat today; it was a big dead deer. Thus the black prey birds hovering around all day yesterday. I called Manny but he said there is nothing to be done. I try to hold my breath when I pass by. This evening a fawn stood on the road not too far from the dead deer. Is it its mother?

Shopping under PA sky always proves to be The More Thing. All those things you don't *really* need, still I buy because *that* is the system here, I shop ergo I live. Or rather I live ergo I shop. The abundance is confusing but tempting, although I was never a great shopper. Still I buy as you can see, can you really? Wineglasses, aren't they pretty? And the plates, simple as you liked. You are surprised I bought myself some flowers. I did because they are beautiful and there is no one else to buy them for me, not that you were a great flower buyer. Not for me, anyway.

On my way today I saw mother goose and small goslings hobbling behind. They didn't run away, just strolled slowly crossing my path. As I left home someone leaped into the forest, a raccoon or maybe a deer.

Something in the grass was glittering and moving this morning. When I looked through my—okay, your—binoculars I saw what looked like lots of white fluttering, I suppose these were chrysalises turning into butterflies. And I saw the bluebirds that probably come every year to nestle here in the special nesting stands by the creek. Blessed be whoever installed them! I follow their flight with the binoculars, so graceful and light and so blue. And the beauty is so sweet and overwhelming it just increases my heartache, why aren't you by my side, my love?

Sitting at my window seat, the sun has set. It's been a hot, humid day. If only Rita would get over her fears. Coming back home this afternoon, I saw again the fawn standing on the road, looking at me, the car really, and then running for its sweet little life.

As you can see our container arrived today. I didn't realize I brought so much stuff. After all, there isn't any furniture, just books and more books, mostly yours, now mine, music, mostly yours and now mine, and souvenirs. I could not leave behind all our photos, your correspondence, your manuscripts and notes. None of your clothes, I gave them all away. Except your winter robe, which I am going to use for the cold. And my clothes you found so dull and unimaginative.

I cannot face unpacking. I sit and sip my wine. I hear you, since when did I become such a wine sipper? Since you died and left some very nice bottles in your tiny wine closet. Now I have wine of my own, which I buy in special stores. This is Pennsylvania, my darling, and you can't find wine or beer in regular stores. Look at the cellar we have in the basement! Cool and wonderful for wine! You would have enjoyed it. Why can't you be happy for me?

How do you like the new furniture? It is the first time I ever chose my own. I don't care if you don't like it. But I did choose it thinking of you. Is it too colorful for you, master of Less Is More? I like it. Look at the dining table, huge and massive, made from a wood similar to the robust beams crisscrossing the barn. So maybe the chairs are a bit too stuffy, but they are very comfortable! You did make me feel that I had no taste. Or that yours was by far superior, and I guess it was, but now I must trust my own. I asked Dea to come with me, but she said, "You are going to have to live with the furniture, you choose," so I did and I think it is beautiful, cozy and simple. The barn is too stunning to spoil with too many things. It stands majestically half empty. I refuse to fall into the American trap of too much of everything! Oh, Alon, don't misunderstand me. I would have preferred shopping with you; I always trusted your taste. But now I am on my own, and I have to build a new life.

Unpacking hurts. I can't look at your photos yet. It is too early. I have only that one photo of yours next to my bed and I am going to put it on my desk. The movers left the boxes with the photos in the basement.

I have a room of my own. I have never had one. I had a desk in our bedroom when we were young and then in the living room, where Dea and her many friends were playing around me while I worked. I am not complaining, I managed and never envied your privacy. Now I chose the most beautiful room, the one you would have most probably designated as your study. I have too many rooms in my barn. Two guestrooms and the ghost wing. Actually I feel as if all the rooms are ghost rooms, full of your presence.

I start putting the books in place, beginning with those you wrote, the hardcovers then paperbacks in all the languages they were translated into. And it is not the dust that makes my eyes tear. I open one of the first you wrote, and there are notes on the side of the pages, passages you highlighted, rewriting your own book. You wrote in other authors' books as well. I never liked that habit of yours, but you said it saves time since you go back to a book and remember your impressions. Actually you were arguing with the writer, improving, editing, and changing shamelessly. So smug, so condescending, so very confident. I was your little opposite. Insecure, self-effacing, humble. I still am. You were impatient with my lack of confidence. But you belittled me, in lots of ways, and I always forgave you, feeling that maybe deep down you were not that confident and that putting me down helped you feel better. Did it really, darling? Was I easier to cope with than challenging Amanda?

It is so hot and muggy up here. There is no air-conditioning on this floor; still, I'd rather have my bedroom and my study here. The small fan I bought doesn't help much. I didn't expect to feel so hot here. They say it is an especially hot and humid summer and that usually it doesn't get so bad. It might be global warming. I will not let it spoil my enchantment!

My desk is ready; your laptop is in working condition. Please, darling, let me concentrate, I need to write my syllabus, I do not have your talent and experience and you can see I am doing everything in my power not to copy yours. On the contrary, I am doing my utmost to keep it as different as I can.

The doorbell rings. Rita barks with all her might. I go down and peep out through the glass side-door: no one. Okay, so I am slightly alarmed, I am alone, and the barn is quite isolated. I go back to my syllabus but the bell rings again. Rita barks throatily, I look out with growing apprehension and see no one. Is it you, my love? I peep through one of the many windows but there is no one in sight. Could someone be hiding and waiting for me to open and then club me dead? So I will join you prematurely and maybe it is not prematurely—they used to burn widows after their husbands' death. You know I wanted to die when you did. I still want to; if I knew for sure I would join you.

The doorbell rings again and you know what, honey, who cares, I will open, and join you NOW. Forget the panic alarm I have. I open the door, my heart pounding hard in my chest. No one. I go up, my heart still racing, and call Manny.

"Oh," he says with nonchalance, "it could be an electrical shortage caused by the humidity."

Humidity!

"Don't worry, Mrs. Whitkin, I will fix the bell tomorrow morning."

Quit saying I am hysterical, Alon, please.

*

Manny indeed came this morning, mowed the grass and fixed the bell and I am sitting here in peace about to complete my syllabus, feeling you hovering around my desk, chuckling. I don't care, Alon. of course you would have done it better, actually you did, but you won't anymore, so please let me be, leave me alone.

Mozart makes it all serene. Yes, darling, I am listening to your CDs but I can call them ours, or mine now. You were haughty when it came to "your" music, but who cares? If I could have you here for one moment, only one, run my hand through your unruly hair, and listen to Mozart with you, I would have died happily afterward.

The doorbell rings, my heart skips a beat. Manny fixed the bell this very morning; can it be the humidity again? I go to the door. Darkness. Rita is barking in frenzy. I remember the outside lights and turn them on. Standing on the porch I see a bunch of half-naked men. I back out automatically planning to get the panic alarm by the bedside. But then I hear a voice, a child's voice crying out, "We're lost!" I summon all my courage and approach the door again. Indeed on the porch there are two men and in front of them two kids half naked, sopping wet and shivering.

I open the door and Rita jumps at the visitors.

I ask them in.

"No," says one of the men, "we will dirty your place, we are full of mud and grass."

"Please come in," I insist, "don't worry about it." My heart, racing like mad just a moment ago, now goes out to the kids. They can't be more than ten.

They come in and stand shaking by the door. Rita is already making friends with them. I rush to the guest bathroom and bring towels. I throw a blanket over the kids and tell them to sit.

"We were rafting," says one of the men, "and we lost our way." I bet. I go to the kitchen and bring the phone.

"Please call your mom!" I tell the kids and they call immediately, I can only guess what is going on in their mother's mind: it is almost ten at night, the sun has set hours ago, and I know the guys here did something irresponsible. It turns out there is more than one mother. The kids are cousins.

"I will never go rafting again," the younger kid promises his mother, hardly containing his tears.

"It was such a relief to see the lights of your house," says the man who wears your beach towel.

"We left while it was still light," apologizes the younger man. "We tried the farmhouse next to you," says the first, "but there was no one there."

"No," I say and decide not to volunteer the information about its being unoccupied.

"We were very afraid when we were rafting and it was dark and we saw nothing at all," says Stan, the older kid.

"Till we saw your lights," says his father and I can only guess *their* fear approaching the isolated barn in the dark, not knowing what to expect. Definitely oblivious to the fact that only a woman and a ghost live here. I am glad they can't see you sneering at me. Gloating at the green stains on my new sofas. The kids play with Rita, who is thrilled by the unexpected company.

"You are safe now," I say, "would you like something to drink?"

"No, no thanks," says John's father.

I bring them some orange juice although they need something warmer.

"We have to be on our way," says Mel.

"Oh, I don't think you can make it, you will have to walk two miles through the forest just to get to the main road. No, I will drive one of you to your car, and you will come back for the rest."

So I am crazy, leaving strangers in the barn, but what can happen? And anyway, you are here, to take care of things, are you not, my darling Alon?

*

I understand Rita's fears better, on our walk today I saw a beautiful animal that looked me in the eyes, then slowly turned around and galloped into the forest, exposing a magnificent bushy reddish tail. I never saw anything like it, I checked the encyclopedia and it was a fox! I realize I have seen it before but didn't know what it was.

I could feel you there at the dean's office today when I signed the contract that was once yours. Of course there were some alterations, I am not and cannot be a writer in residence, or his surviving widow, no, I am an expert on language and literature. You saw I was more surprised than you could ever be. Please don't say it, it isn't fair. It was not pity. Why should anyone offer me a job—okay, your job—out of pity? Spring College is not a charitable institution. This is the USA, why should anyone care if you were blown into tiny pieces? They have their own problems.

I wonder what kind of students I'll have. I told the dean "Most likely every student in my class speaks English better than I do." And he said, "Don't count on it." It is not the course you were going to teach, do you feel better now? Most of my students are freshmen;

yours were supposed to be graduates. Who knows, maybe they would have offered me the job even if you were alive. I suppose they would have. If and if, this is not a good time to bring it all up, Alon. I start teaching after the weekend, I am not ready yet, and I am scared. Very. I never spoke in public. I hear you, it is not a public, it is a class, but you were at home in classrooms, I am not. Why, I don't think I was in one since I graduated long ago. What am I going to tell these kids? I will feel your eminent presence around me. Envy your ease when you were addressing a public, any public. Knowing in advance you are going to charm them all, especially the women. Your famous charisma was blown to pieces as well. So how come you are still here, lingering in the growing shadows, making me feel small, unimportant, insignificant, a failure? You will always be here, there, everywhere, for good and for worse till death us unite. Go away, Alon. I need to work. I don't feel ready yet although I wrote pages and pages, consulted books in our library, even read your notes, trying to find out what you planned to teach your classes. How on earth am I going to stay away from your huge shadow? Stop hovering. Sorry, darling, I didn't mean it. It is just that dead or alive I cannot shake you off. It is as if you go on living through me, breathing into and out of my lungs.

I am going to leave you here, in our big, beautiful renovated barn. You are not allowed to follow me outside. I will tell you everything when I get back, but please let me do this on my own without making me feel you would have done it so much better. How can you go on being so powerful even after death?

I know I am giving you the power, but I suppose I can't do otherwise. Yet.

*

I am so happy to see her, our beautiful, self-confident, wise daughter. She arrives without losing her way once, driving from New York City. Embracing me, she looks around with your deep blue critical eyes, but I can see her approval.

"This is gorgeous!"

Rita yelps at her all excited. They dance together as they used to when they were both younger.

I follow Dea as she strolls from room to room, appraising, admiring, marveling.

"Oh, mom, this is lovelier than I imagined! It is paradise. But aren't you scared to be so remote and alone out in the woods?"

"No, I am not," I say, I don't think I can tell her you are here looking after me in your overbearing way. She stops at my bedside, looking gravely at your picture.

"He must be younger than I am now," she comments.

"No, he just looked young. He was older than you are now when we first met."

She turns around, looks me in the eyes. "Do you regret having met him?"

I am taken by surprise, I never thought about it that way. Our meeting was so obvious to me as if I have been waiting for you all my previous life.

"No, sweetheart, if I hadn't met Dad you wouldn't have been born, right?"

She goes on looking in my eyes. "I mean for you, for your life."

"I don't know, I never think about it."

"Never mind." She shrugs. She goes into my study and looks around. She reaches out and caresses the books. Your books.

"You can have any book you want," I say at once.

"I know." She reads the titles, still caressing them. She gets to the shelf with the children books I brought as well. She takes out *The Little Prince* in Hebrew. "Can I take this one? Dad used to read it to me so often."

"Of course," I say, "it is on my syllabus."

"Is it really? So you will need it."

"Not in Hebrew."

She hugs the book. "I miss him," she says sadly.

"So do I," fighting back my tears.

She hugs me. I hug her.

"You must be starving," and we go down arm in arm.

Dea explores the basement with starry eyes.

"When I come over for a weekend I'll sleep here."

"But there is nothing here, no bed, no bathroom."

"I don't mind."

"I thought you were going to stay the night."

"I have to be back in the city," she says, avoiding my eyes.

She wants to go out to the pastures immediately and Rita joins her trotting happily at her heel. I go along, watching them run together used to each other's pace, advancing towards the creek, and I feel a stab of pain, you would have run with them, teasing them both, joining in, being part of their intimacy. I trail behind thinking about the cookies I made for Dea's breakfast. She stops in her tracks, turns around and says, "Mom! Get going!"

They wait for me, I arrive slightly out of breath and Dea takes my arm, "Hey, Mom, don't be sad! You got yourself a magical place!"

"You are right," I say, squeezing her arm.

We follow Rita, who gains more confidence with us around, venturing to the water edge, sniffing the water and sipping some.

"You look well," says Dea, gazing at the water.

"I do?"

"Yes. Much better. I think you did the right thing."

I say nothing, but am glad she approves. She wanted me to come here from the very beginning, encouraging me when my determination faltered.

"I think you are going to be a hell of a teacher," she says.

I think I blush. "Honest?"

"Honest, Mom." She squeezes my arm.

We stroll back to the barn and I feel happier than I have in a long time. Coming from the creek the house looks overpowering, big and magnificent. I feel proud.

It is a beautiful day; the sky is blue and everything in sight so very green. I am toying with the idea of spreading our lunch on a blanket in the meadow but the wasps buzz around and chase away such notions.

We go up to the living room, Dea rushes to the window seat. "A deer!" she exclaims excitedly. "And another one!"

"You are lucky; usually they don't come out during the day, just around sunset or sunrise."

"Of course I am lucky," she says, the exact same words and intonation you would have used, full of self-confidence.

She turns to face the dining table. "It is divine!" she exclaims. "How appropriate! It is so much like the beams!"

I am beaming with pleasure. She looks at all the goodies I set on our lovely dining table.

"Oh, Mom, you always exaggerate!"

"You are my first visitor here." We both know I would have prepared the same things for her anyway, but she says nothing.

Everything she likes is here. Humus, tahina, falafel, eggplant. No meat, since she became vegetarian years ago.

"You baked my cheesecake!"

We sit on both sides of the table I realize is too big for two. She eats with great appetite and I enjoy looking at her.

"Do you dream about Dad?" she asks all of a sudden.

"No."

"Well, maybe it is too early, although I did. Last night."

She goes on eating in silence, sipping her lemonade.

"What was the dream about?" I ask carefully, fearing she might not want to share it with me.

"He was waiting for me on a platform, could have been a train station. He looked cheerful. He hugged me and said, 'Welcome.'" She stops.

"And?"

"That was all."

"Maybe you were thinking about coming here and—"

She interrupts me: "Yes, that's what I think, as if he was waiting for me here."

"He is here," I say very quietly.

"I know," she says, "but I hope you will let him go one day? Soon?"

"Should I?"

"Yes. You are the one holding on to him."

She sees my tears before I realize they are there, gets up, comes toward me, puts her hands on my shoulders and says, "I am sorry, Mom, I know it's too early."

"Too early for what?"

"For letting him go."

I am not sure I understand her, maybe I don't want to and maybe yes, our wise daughter is right, it is too early for me to let go. To let go of you and the enormous place you occupied and still occupy in my life.

I wipe my tears with the back of my hand; Dea returns to her chair.

"I am seeing someone," she says out of the blue, Dea, who never shares much with me. I wait silently for her to go on, but she is busy savoring her baba genouch.

"You look happy," I say at last.

"I am," she says. "He reminds me of Dad."

"Is that good or bad?" We both laugh.

"I don't know," she says, puts her fork down and gazes at the pasture she is facing. "He is very confident and sometimes childish. He is stubborn and opinionated and doesn't like criticism."

"He does sound like your dad and…like you."

"Right," she says and resumes eating.

This is one thing I couldn't get away with in the past with either of you. You and Dea couldn't take criticism very well. She is changing, growing, something you can't do anymore and didn't when you were still alive.

"Tell you what: I will bring him over for a weekend as soon as we both can manage some free time."

"Good." I have lots of questions I want to ask, all the questions you would have asked, like what does he do, how old is he, what kind of family he comes from, parents' questions, but I don't dare, remembering well Dea's way of putting me off with "it is none of your business" answers.

"I love you," I blurt out all of a sudden, surprising us both equally. She looks at me astonished, her mouth full of cheesecake. I feel the tears mounting again and to stop them I sip lemonade.

Dea manages to swallow her food and says, "I love you too, Mom."

I nod, not trusting my voice.

"You are going to be fine," she says. "I wasn't sure for a while, after Dad died I thought you might never recuperate, but seeing you here"—she motions with her arm the room around us—"I am positive you will be better off than you were with him."

"What do you mean? I was very happy with Dad!"

"Were you really?"

I say nothing, thinking hard.

"You were always stressed. Always apprehensive because of Dad. Afraid to upset him. Afraid to oppose him. Afraid to lose him."

"And I did!"

"No, I mean lose him in a different way."

I know what she means at once, and I don't want her to say it.

"I am sorry; I don't want to distress you. It is just that I worry about you. That is why I didn't come to see you earlier."

"I don't understand."

"I was afraid you were going to become an eternal widow. Glorifying Dad and his atrocious death. Sort of idealizing him and keeping a distorted image of him. Oh, Mom, we all know he was no angel."

"No, he wasn't."

And strangely enough we both laugh and if you are a fly on the wall, Alon darling, too bad for you!

*

I hardly slept at night; my throat is parched, my heart racing like mad when I enter my first class. It is so quiet I think maybe there is no one there, but the students are at their places, sitting quietly, waiting for me. I smile a shaky smile, say, "Good morning," and ask them to pick up their chairs and arrange them in a circle. They seem surprised but they comply. It gives me a moment to pull myself together. We all sit in a circle, I look at them, they look expectantly at me. I introduce myself and ask them to introduce themselves. They are obviously shy. They each say their name, and are at a loss for any other words of introduction. I don't insist, I look at their open faces and relax. It is going to be fine.

I teach my first class, trying not to look at my notes. I talk about literature, in general, trying to define it, to prove that actually everything is literature, or can be made so. I find myself improvising, entertaining, performing; I never knew I had it in me. I tell them analyzing literature is less important than loving and enjoying reading. I say I am going to do my very best to make them fall in love with books.

It is going to be tough to memorize all the names; so I ask them to find a protagonist who bears their name, someone with more similarities than just the name. They write down their assignment, I advise them to search in the library or online, and offer my help in case they don't find such a character. It is an improvisation, and I don't have time to discover the source of my inspiration.

It is easier than I anticipated. It goes so smoothly I feel an immense relief when the class is over. It is exhilarating, and the beauty of it is that I never once thought about you, I was far too busy with my students! I am already looking forward to my next class, buzzing with new and exciting ideas.

And frankly, my dear, I don't care how *you* would have taught them!

Okay, I do care, but I have some notion, and more, about how you taught. Let us never forget I was—for a while—your student. You were flamboyant in class. Full of verve and fire. You never sat down; you were dancing all over the place, using hands, arms, your incredibly flexible face. You were a storm the first time I saw you, a dramatic actor, you were what you taught, passionate about it, so knowledgeable and in deep need of kudos and applause. No wonder I fell in love with you, as did most students, women and men. I still don't know why you chose me when you could have had someone more charismatic, intelligent or prettier. Yes, I know Amanda was all these and so much more, so you probably needed someone less glamorous, less threatening, more out of your league, so that you would not have to face competition again. I know you know she called yesterday and said hesitantly she would like to visit sometime. I can see your discomfort, your first wife meeting your second without you around, are we going to compare notes? I don't think so. Neither of us is made of that stuff, but who knows, you might enjoy it postmortem. I will not lie to you: I am apprehensive. I always was when it comes to Amanda, your beautiful, achieved and achieving first wife, so very different from your dull, simple study in contrast second one.

Last time we met was at your funeral. She flew in especially. At first I thought she wanted to be there for Benjamin, but he didn't come. She said he couldn't cope with your death. She says he still is in great pain. I asked her to bring him along with her when she comes, but she was evasive, said he is too busy now that he is a father himself. I dare not tell her you were rehearsing the grandfather's role: "Don't call me Grandpa, call me Alon," afraid to grow old, frowning at each wrinkle and silver hair. So now you have it, you are not going to grow old and your grandson was born after you died.

When will I stop arguing with you in my head? The therapist said I might spill out lots of things I kept buried now that you are. Buried. Sorry, darling, I don't know what has gotten into me. I guess I never got over Amanda, although she was the first and I the second. Maybe it is precisely that.

I am taking Rita out through the basement door—there are five of them—she is stamping toward the cornfield. She loves running in the furrows with the corn around her, so much higher, why, it is my height now and I am not on the short side. I can't wait for the little ears to grow so that I can boil or grill them. I bought some corn and loved it; it is so much softer and sweeter than the corn back home. But so are so many other things here! Could I be vilifying my homeland on purpose, so that I can better adapt to my new home, or has Israel really become such a vile place? I guess both. As a way of justifying being here and being so happy about it and yes, it has become a vile place where one's husband can leave in the morning and never come back because a terrorist has decided to take him away with her to what she conceives as heaven. I am not going to indulge in self-pity and cry, not if I look at the beauty around me, have you ever seen a more splendid weeping willow than the one perching over the little farmhouse next door? I have tender feelings toward the humbler, cozier and so graceful empty neighboring house. In a way it would have suited me better, but the barn was so much like you: big, overpowering, domineering, self-confident, majestic. Don't misunderstand, I love the barn. I never lived in a more dramatically magnificent house. Still, it is much too big for me. I don't think I can afford it longer than a year but I refuse to think about it now.

The silence, the serenity, the utter splendor of this place is a balm on my pain and loss, It appeases me, erases a big part of my tormented memory, heals me.

*

I am fumbling with my keys, all new and shining. The key to the barn, the car key, and the last arrival, the key to my tiny office on campus. Yes, I have a somewhat ascetic room, but with time I will turn it into a gem!

Entering my second class is less scary. Again my students are sitting quietly; they already arranged their chairs in a circle.

I talk to them some more about the power of words, and then ask them to read their assignments. I am getting to know Rebecca, who chose the biblical protagonist since she too believes that being a wife and a mother is important. She reads a passage that reveals Rebecca's wisdom.

Catherine reads from *Wuthering Heights* describing Cathy's stay at the Thrushcross Grange, learning some manners, "fine clothes and flattery" turning her into a "very dignified person." Catherine chose this protagonist since she, too, was a wild kid and has, with time, become more disciplined. Dorothy chose the *Wizard of Oz* and says this is her all-time favorite book and movie. She identifies with Dorothy as she too believes there is no place like home, but sometimes you have to leave in order to appreciate it. We discuss their feelings being away from home, most of the students come from close-by areas, and still it is their first time away from home. I relate to my class that in Hebrew we say "First night without Mom" referring to the first day of military service. While I talk and see their eyes widen in surprise I realize how farfetched mandatory military service sounds to them. I know this too can change.

To my delight Alexandra chose Lillian Hellman's *The Little Foxes*. She reads, in a very little voice, the end of the play, when Alexandra flies away from her mother, explaining she is not going to stand around and watch her eating earth. Alexandra says she feels that way living on her own, away from her overprotective mother. Maya chose Maya Angelou's *Singin' and Swingin' and Getting Merry like Christmas*. In a lovely deep voice she reads a passage describing Maya's first performance as a dancer. She chose the book because she too likes to sing and dance. She is auditioning for a musical the college is about to stage.

I keep urging the students to comment, compliment, or say something about their fellow students' choices, but to no avail. It seems participation is not something the students here are used to. I blush remembering how I said on the first class that the only ground rule I have is respecting one another's opinion and never interrupting. It seems that at Spring College Pennsylvania it is redundant.

Chris chose Robert M. Pirsig's *Zen and the Art of Motorcycle Maintenance*. I am thrilled; it was one of our favorites when we first read it. Of course, the son's name was Chris. He reads a passage about the motorcycle and explains he rides one and therefore chose the book although he admits he didn't read the whole book—"The librarian recommended it" he says. They don't read as much as we did when we were their age.

Driving back home, I am reflecting for the first time on my name. I never questioned it, never thought about it; never "adopted" it the way I asked my students to re-choose their own names.

You loved Daphne's mythological story. Have you ever stopped to think about the real significance of my name? Daphne was so reluctant to Apollo's love she turned into a laurel bush, into Daphne, the Hebrew word for laurel bush and spice. Did you realize how terrorized she was at the prospect of physical love? She preferred turning into a bush, though she consented to serve as a wreath to Apollo's and other heroes' heads. I always felt you weren't attracted to me, I felt inadequate sexually, I still do. So you see how suitable my name is?

It is sheer bliss driving down the dirt road, my dirt road. Mine and the deer's and the raccoons'. My little Bambi is waiting in its usual spot. Yes, the dead deer was its mother. The smell is fading slowly but I still hold my breath when I pass.

Rita barks and jumps on me, she is lonely all day, and I put down my grocery bags and take her for a stroll. The birds are singing their evening mass, a beautiful, soaring song that melts my heart and reminds me how much I miss you. But I am setting these thoughts aside, trying to enjoy the here and now. How can one not? The pastures are glorious; their translucent greenness hurts my eyes. I don't want to get used to the beauty, to take it for granted. I hear a cry coming from the woods; can it be a cuckoo-bird? My mother used to say that hearing a cuckoo cry brings luck. These are not tears, silly, just the sunshine in my eyes and seeing you so very clearly, as if you were here by my side walking your Marguerita. Sure enough, Rita sees a squirrel and chases it as if she has been doing so all her life. The forest around is slightly less threatening, and I suppose that in due course she will start venturing out on her own.

I am not hungry yet, so I take my wine up to the library and browse the books. It is becoming a habit, each evening I find another book you have possessed, made your own by corresponding with its writer. I am reading your too-many-to-count notes and it is as if I am corresponding with you beyond death. I go to your favorites; yesterday it was Kafka, tonight it is Stendhal. My dear Alon, you were actually arguing with all of them. Correcting, improving their writings! So what does it make you? Better than Kafka? Than Stendhal? You argued with your own books as well, feeling you could constantly improve them. I know that was the way you taught your admiring students. I was one of them. Nabokov, remember? Pronounced NA-Vo-Koff as you always insisted. He was *our* first writer. How appropriate. To this very date. Look at me: I have become our cherished Pnin. A foreigner teaching at a college just like him, maybe as pathetic. Only he had Nabokov himself, his writer and creator, later on destroying his career and his life. Maybe the way you would have done if...if you weren't dead. Remember we used to quote Nabokov quoting Pushkin's reminiscing about his own death: "In fight, in travel, or in waves?" He died in a stupid duel. Is a bomb dumber than a duel? It is probably the same thing, both a vanity game made by man. Right, the porter of your suicide bomb was a woman but she was playing according to men's rules. Revenging her brother, her fiancé, both? I am not going to cry. So it hurts, but look at me: I am becoming good at cynicism, almost as good as you were, but not as vicious.

Did I tell you about the nights at the barn? When it's clear you can count all the stars, you can distinguish every one of them and you knew their names and could talk about each one at length. I remember lying in your arms at the beach and while you explained, demonstrated and lectured on and on and I just wanted you to lean over and kiss me, but I listened all smitten, madly in love, praying the dream would never end. Little did I know one bomb was going to blow this dream into pieces. Or was it the bomb? I refuse to think about it. Look at the moon, how beautiful she rises behind the trees, so majestically, blushing slightly, as though waiting for applause.

*

I get up a bit later, no teaching today. Time on my own to savor. I will read the students' essays, make some phone calls, catch up with my reading, but right now I push the shutters wide open and gaze out at the green-green meadow, still shining from the rain's scrub, at the lush forest behind the creek busily overflowing. Two graceful deer graze nearby, their white tails waving cheerfully. Birds by the dozens are resting on the river's shore, before taking flight, all of a sudden, in a colorful flutter.

I can hear Rita yelping at my door, demanding her meal, in a while; I just want to soak in the splendor and feel it in my veins like a potent, soothing drug. Maybe you can't grasp peace, real harmony and serenity until you experience war and its wounds. Rita is quite oblivious to these facts and insists on her more immediate needs. I put on my sneakers, ready for our walk.

We go out by one of the basement's doors; Rita gallops away maybe as homage to the horses that once used to gallop out of these doors. The deer have vanished; Rita sniffs around, guessing their presence. For all I know she could be smelling you, my unseen presence. Am I being frivolous? I don't think so. I will never make light of your death, but in order to survive I must learn to let go and I don't think I am doing too well. Yet.

I listen to the morning's symphony. The crickets sound off-key, as if they are tuning their instruments, the birds are busy humming their chirpy tunes, and small insects buzz about industriously, all accompanying the creek's soft murmur. I cannot think of a better music to my ears. And I don't mind being stung—again—by famished female mosquitoes. The female is the biting one. Again a matter of survival. Of the fittest?

Home we trot, Rita and I, anticipating breakfast.

I sit at my comfy window seat enjoying the view and my freshly brewed espresso, yes, my darling; I am indulging my senses or what's left of them after your insensible death. I know I should feel guilty, but I don't. No, sweetheart, not because of you, but because I have so much work to do and I am sprawled between my soft pillows, letting the loveliness gratify my eyes, all my senses.

With all the willpower I can muster I get up and go up to my study, not forgetting to caress the stunning wood beams on my way, trying to imagine the farmers who put them together with dedication decades ago.

I sit in my reclining chair, lean back and breathe deeply. No more excuses, I have to work. The screen lights up, I enter my e-mail. Junk. A word from Nell, saying she is in a rush and will write later. The *New York Times*. Okay, I will browse. And there it is, red on white; it is my mind that goes black.

A suicide bomb in Jerusalem. Someone crazy in me wants to shut down the screen at once, erase the news as you kill the messenger, and annihilate the deed as if it didn't happen. Most of me knows this is real and was expected all along. And a small voice says, *Rejoice it didn't happen so far.* But I am already busy reading and searching, clicking the Hebrew news, frantically trying to remember who lives next to the bomb site, and all the while the voice of the trauma therapist shouts in my mind, it is going to come back to you with every explosion.

I realize I am crying when I see the tears splashing the keyboard. I can't stop, I am shaking all over. How could I have this lazy coffee sitting stupidly at the window, daydreaming while this has been going on? A few hours have elapsed since it happened, and I didn't know. They already identified two bodies. Young students on their way to school.

And suddenly it is all back. Your bomb. It resonates in my ears as it did then, all those months ago. Vibrating through me, shattering me again. I was unsuspicious then as I was this morning. Only when the hours passed and your cell phone didn't respond did the slightest suspicion creep into my mind and grew and grew, climaxing with the atrocious certainty of identifying your remains. It is all so vivid. How could I have believed it was fading?

The piercing ring makes me jump. I pick up the phone with trembling hands, my throat parched, my heart beating fast. I try to say hello but my voice betrays me.

"Mom?"

I sob all over the phone.

"So you know," she says. I nod, as if she can see.

"I just found out," she says out of breath.

"Me too," I manage to mumble.

"I am sorry," she says, and I know she is crying too.

"You don't have to worry about Grandma, I just called her, and she is fine."

Of course, Erica, I didn't even have time to think about her. She lives next to the site. As does Dad, how could I forget?

"Mom?"

"Oh, Dea."

"Do you want me to come over?"

"No, darling, I will be okay. It's just; just…it is a shock."

"I know."

"Everything comes back, as if it never left. I have been living in a fool's paradise."

"No, Mom. It is not true. It's just too soon and you knew Dad's wasn't the last one."

We don't say the words. Suicide bomb. It is too painful. But we feel the same way. They said time and again that the wound is going to bleed every time there will be another unexpected bomb. And when I stop to think about it, it is so expected. It is not over. And even that bomb is not the last one, an unbearable thought.

"Would you like to come to New York? We can have dinner together."

"No, sweetie, I have some work." How on earth will I be able to work?

A third name pops up on the screen. I watch compulsively the horrible photos, almost regretting not having a TV so I could see even more explicit pictures from the scene.

"I have to go," says Dea, "I need to make some phone calls, will call you later. Will you be okay, Mom?" There is a plea in her voice.

I pull myself together as best as I can.

"I will be okay, sweetie, we'll talk later."

The phone slides out of my hand and I gaze at the screen with unseeing eyes.

And I thought I was recuperating. Surviving. Healing. The pain in my chest is excruciating. Dad is the only person I want to talk to right now. How come he hasn't called so far?

I dial his number with shaking hands. Not stopping to wonder who is making the call, the child needing consolation or the adult anxious to hear her aging father's voice.

He answers at once: "Is it you, Daphne?"

"Yes."

We keep silent for a while and I listen to the somewhat reassuring crackles on the long-distance line.

"Why didn't you call me at once?" I ask at last.

"I didn't want to wake you up."

"I was not asleep," I say daftly. Of course I was asleep when it happened. There are seven whole hours separating us.

"Listen, it is going to get easier."

"From bomb to bomb?" a shot of cynicism.

"Yes," he says with his grave baritone voice I always find comforting.

"Well, I am not there yet."

"No," he says. "How is teaching?" he asks, obviously wanting to change the subject.

"Fine," I say, "so far."

"Dea?" he asks in his shorthand style.

"Okay. She just called. She spoke with Erica and she is okay."

"Everyone we know is okay, I think," he says.

"So when are you coming?" I ask the same question every time we talk on the phone and he always says, "Soon."

"Soon, kid. When are you coming?"

"Not before the…the memorial."

"I thought you might have changed your mind."

"Why should I? I love it here, except…"

"Except there is nowhere to run to."

He and I have been there time and again. He believes with all his generous warm aging heart that the only place for Jews is Israel and even a dead son-in-law, a victim of hostile acts, as they call it officially, did not change his mind. And the Holocaust is what formed his mind.

"Are you alone?" he asks.

"Of course I am," I say. He is the last one who needs to know about ghosts and apparitions.

"It is not good." I can see him shaking his balding head.

"Dad!" Mother died twelve years ago and he is still on his own.

"Okay, child, you know what's right." Do I really?

"I will write," I promise. Dad doesn't believe in virtual communication. He writes me real letters on paper, with his fountain pen, folded carefully into envelopes with colorful stamps oblivious to the time each letter takes to arrive. His letters are in very solemn biblical Hebrew only foreigners to the language can adopt. From time to time I write back. Always short for words. Writing real letters seems to me like something from the past.

"Do you eat well?" he asks, a typical father question.

"Of course I do," and I almost smile but on the screen in front of me I see live pictures from the explosion scene. Strange how they all look alike. And smell, they all smell like hot blood, smoke and charred flesh. I shudder.

"Bye, Dad, take care."

"You too," and he hangs up quickly, before blurting out something emotional that is absolutely against his secular religion.

I am sitting gaping into the bloody screen without really seeing it, while in my mind's eyes the terrible pictures run like an intact vivid movie, the bomb and then the amazing deep, undisturbed total silence that follows the explosion. And then hell breaks loose, people screaming, others sobbing, wounded starting their agony among the carnage, while the bodies, of killed and killer, lie torn to bits and pieces, mingled all around the bleeding inferno scene. A few minutes and then sirens begin to tear the air, screeching for their life, and others' lives, coming from all directions at once.

And although this has happened time and again, for years now, the atrocity, the horror, the utter dreadfulness doesn't lose heart- and gut-wrenching disbelief. *No way to live no way to die.* And amid all the ambulances, fire engines, police, avid press, the black and yellow ZAKA—the squadron collecting human parts—whose name in Hebrew means "Truth," there is an overwhelming feeling of despair and powerlessness.

And it is precisely that very feeling I thought I overcame. Stupid me. It is all over me again with a vengeance. I am powerless, numb, distressed, helpless and hapless. Depressed and desperate.

Oh, back then I was full of life. For a while. Till the atrocious certitude sunk in. But at first I called your cell phone and your office till my fingers were numb. Later came the hospitals, whose numbers were on all screens, they are on right now in front of me. Special numbers keep blinking, available for worried-out-of-their-minds family members. I wasn't alone. By then Edna was with me and Dad and some of your colleagues and students, who for hours expected you at the university in vain. Our house became headquarters run by Ram, your colleague and best friend.

Then followed the hospital grand tour. To all of them. Reading lists of names. Hoping you are there on one of the many improvised beds, smiling your sarcastic smile and asking, "What's all the fuss about? So I got some burns, no big deal." I was bargaining with the God I never acknowledge, I was willing to give up so much! Your eyes, a leg, a hand, maybe even two; I was more than willing to sit months beside your bed, as long as you were going to live. Strangely enough I was not crying, too busy hoping and praying. *Please, please, please, don't let him die. I will do anything.* I am ashamed to recall I was even willing to become a born-again Jew and respect the Sabbath if only you were okay. I see your grin, Alon. I was ready then and still am now; I would give anything just to have you alive.

The phone numbers of the hospitals blip on the screen, probably the same numbers we called not so long ago, before giving up the busy lines and driving there ourselves. Driving from one hospital to the next, I felt as if parts of me were dying. I couldn't talk, I couldn't breathe. Everyone around treated me as if I was made out of the most fragile china; some still think I am a teacup.

The last hospital was Hadassah; most of the wounded were there. I was too weak to walk and sat on the bench in the trauma center waiting for Ram. I knew the moment he averted his eyes from mine. I knew what was in store but couldn't pronounce the words. Something in me was screaming, *It is not true, he is alive.* Edna once said I shouted out loud these words but I have no recollection of it.

I knew where we were heading before we hit the road. And still with shaking fingers I tried to dial your cell phone, hoping with all my might you would answer.

In my mind I can see the families that are at this very moment on their way to the cursed place, the one from which there is no return.

No way to live no way to die. The final station on this Via Dolorosa. Last stop, tearing doubt turns into certainty, hope crushes forever. The ultimate identification.

The scene is here now. I relive it with cutting clarity. I am there in my mind, in my heart, in every aching muscle and nerve I have. There again with all the other families, sitting at the Pathological Institute for Juridical Medicine in Abu Kabir, a name that makes one shudder, the cursed place where body parts are assembled and family members identify the remains of their loved ones.

I don't remember getting there; Ram and Edna drove me over. Held my hand. Wiped my sweating forehead, heard me howl. What I do remember is the waiting, the bloodcurdling vacillation between life and death, hope and realization. I can still hear my name called—no, it was your name. As if it was you they were calling. And since you were not there to get up, I did, trembling, leaning on the anonymous psychologist, one of many, who were there for this horrible march into the morgue, a march I haven't ended yet and will not till I join you there.

Oh, they were so very considerate and trained, experienced bomb after bomb. They didn't show me your torn parts. They were probably impossible to separate from the others'; including the woman's who blew you all up. But they did show me your purse, torn beyond recognition with shreds of your ID and credit cards, and something under a green sheet. I didn't look at it, I couldn't. I just looked into Ram's eyes, begging wordlessly, *Should I look?* And he shook his head and hugged me. I often wondered if I should have looked, but I trust Ram. It wasn't a sight to see. I don't even know which part he saw to identify you. All I needed to know was that it was you and that there was no doubt about it, although I would have traded anything to have the benefit of a doubt, but it was not granted. Ram told the MD in green clothes, "It is him," and that was it.

I turn my eyes for the first time to the oblivious outside, almost defying the beauty to dare challenge my torment. And it does without shame, the sun coming out behind the clouds and drowning the scenery with light and splendor.

I cry as I soak in the appeasing sights, feeling as if my haven has been contaminated.

The phone rings. I pick it up and say a shaky hello.

"It's Amanda."

"Amanda," I repeat mechanically.

"So you heard."

She sounds shaky as well. "I am sorry," she says.

I want to say, *It is not your fault*, but I don't.

"It is terrible."

"It is."

"And it brings it all back."

"It does."

"Erica is okay."

"I know, Dea called her." As okay as a mother who lost a son in a previous suicide bomb can be.

"I just wanted to…I don't know." Amanda, short for words!

"Is Benjamin okay?"

"Yes, he heard about it and called me."

"It is very considerate of you to think of me."

"I think a lot about you," she says at once.

I have the impulse to ask, *Why?* but I curb it. I don't tell her I think a lot about her as well.

"If there is anything I can do…"

I don't say, *It is too late.* I just say, "When is all this going to end?"

I can hear her shrug.

"This is not a way to live," she says, the exact words you used to say. This is not a way to die either.

"Thanks, Amanda," is all I say.

"Take care," she says and we both hang up hesitantly.

I have a message on the screen. Edna is trying to call but the line is busy. I write back saying briefly I am okay under the circumstances and not to worry; we will talk some time tomorrow or during the weekend. There is nothing I want to say or hear that I didn't say or hear before and right now I need the silence of the barn to engulf me and soothe me and allow me to take again deep breaths and come back to life as it was before, if that is possible.

*

Lately I am too numb to listen, to my barn and its breathtaking musical surroundings, to my friends on the phone, to the first whispers of fall, even to my students. I am just putting one foot in front of the other, going through the motions; my feelings are on an automated pilot. I missed most of the talk about the coming hurricane with a romantic woman's name.

But even I hear about her at last, and realize everyone is preparing for the onslaught.

"What does one do?" I ask Karen, my colleague who has her office across the corridor from mine.

"Well," she says, shrugging. "I guess get ready."

I refrain from telling her I have seen worse, that after my own hurricane, who incidentally had a woman's name as well, nothing much can scare me.

"So how does one get ready for a hurricane?" I ask Karen.

"You stock up on food, candles and stuff."

Lots of e-mails from the campus safety predict all kind of terrible scenarios. They are debating whether the college will stay open.

So on my way home I stop by the store and shop for a flashlight, some candles, matches and food that can't go bad in case of blackout.

I drive and think that Mother Nature's calamities are not half as threatening as human calamities, not because they are more predictable, which they are not, but because there are no feelings behind it, no agenda whatsoever. Natural disasters do not happen in order to punish or take revenge, they do not mean to destroy or hurt, let alone kill. Nature is utterly indifferent and indiscriminating to human's fate or ordeal; it is sometimes a predictable result of changing pressures, temperatures or streams. Nothing more.

And although we know it is coming, there is nowhere to hide, which consoles me. In a way I wish the barn will crumble over me, the wild winds will carry me, the creek will flood, and I will join you. I am entitled to my puerile thoughts.

Once in the barn, I feel sheltered, the way this place always makes me feel. I call Dea.

"I am fine," she reassures me, "but what about you?"

"What about me?"

"I don't know, all alone in the middle of nowhere. What if something happens to you?"

"Like what?"

"I don't know, Mom, maybe you should have come here."

"I will be fine, don't worry, I am well prepared."

Thank heaven she doesn't ask how or what for. I promise to call her as soon as possible, meaning that if the power is off, I will call once it's back.

I scatter the candles in different places around the house, just in case, and go in the kitchen to cook. I tell myself that if the anticipated power cut will come, I will be ready. At least I will not starve. The connection between food and disaster is tight. Growing up in a home where Holocaust trauma was at all times present, food was pretty much part of it. There was no throwing away food. Food was survival, period. You had to finish everything on your plate, not because there were hungry children around the world, but because in the camps there was no food. Period. I never argued. Being an only child I couldn't revolt, and the idea never crossed my mind. My role was not to upset my parents, who have been upset for several lifetimes. Period.

And then you came along and I found myself spending hours in the kitchen doing my best to impress you. I don't think I succeeded. I always felt Amanda was a better cook, better in so many other areas, but I never gave up trying. So yes, I brought with me my ample cookbook collection. But now I am improvising and since you are not going to taste any of it, I trust my instincts without referring to written recipes.

Look at me; I will never learn to cook for one. I cook as if a hungry battalion is on its way. The fear of not having enough. Rita will appreciate it in the coming days. If we make it, she and I.

I tune to the Weather Channel on my radio. Warnings and more warnings. I am not intimidated. On the contrary, I feel a slight excitement. My only regret is that you are not here with me. If the deluge is coming the way they are prophesying better be a couple like in old Noah's ark. But I don't need an end of the world prediction in order to miss you so violently. Well, one miserable consolation, I don't have to worry about your safety any longer. A relief made in hell, don't you think?

I am trying to guess what we would have done if you were here. I don't believe we would have escaped elsewhere. Where to? No. You would have sat in your reclining chair, intertwining your gracious fingers—God, do I miss them—behind your neck and laughed, no doubt, yes, you would have made fun of my stupid preparations. The way you did before and during both Gulf wars, when I was busy setting up the sealed room, with all the food I could lay my hands on.

I sit and await the impending disaster. I can hear the wind blowing hard, not only against the windows and the trees around the house, but it also growls in the empty fireplace and in the oven, even the microwave is rattling. All of a sudden everything outside is lit like daylight. My heart beats faster. It can't be a power interruption, right, and it is too long for lightning. I summon my courage and look closely out the window. I don't see the source of light but the whole place is lit like a movie set. Rita barks hysterically, most likely mirroring my alarm. A flying saucer is about to land outside my door, and I am here alone! I can see the title: *Space Rafters in a PA Barn!*

"Okay," I say out loud, frightening further Rita and myself. "Out we go."

I open the door hesitantly and Rita and I step outside. Big mistake, the wind is about to blow the door shut. I run for my keys and step out with more determination. Big projectors on both sides of the barn are on. Did I push any button I haven't so far? I am not going to call Manny right now, I am sure he is busy with his own hurricane.

What the hell, I tell myself, if I am out, better turn it into an adventure. Worst-case scenario, I'll join you sooner than expected.

"Let's go and see how the creek is doing," I tell Rita.

The wind blows hard and I think that if I were frailer I could be flying. The air is full with other flying objects, mainly from the cornfield; I hope this is not going to ruin the crops.

The creek is raging; ripples hurry furiously, flurry white crests, streaming on faster than I ever saw it. Rita clings to my leg. Lightning strikes, are you there, Alon? And then a thunder rolls, swallowing all other sound, including the crazy beat of my heart.

I know I am irresponsible toward Rita, and she looks at me with blaming eyes. "We have been through worse," I tell her, but the wind snaps my words, slaps my hair on my face and makes me gasp for air. Okay, Marguerita, home we go, but the wind is against us, pushing us back to the creek. I snap up Rita before the wind does and force my way back to our mansion, still lit as if on stage.

The radio is reporting disasters; ravages and floods caused by Her Majesty the Hurricane on Her wild chase, here and in nearby states.

I eat the stew huddled in my window seat, Rita by my side, sharing bites and pieces. The good wine is just for me. I drink a second glass tonight, one for Rita, and the third one for you. It could be my last supper.

The projectors are still lit, making the whole scene surreal, but awesome. I don't know why, but I go up and a bit unsteadily put on the CD with Renata Tebaldi singing Desdemona's swan song in Verdi's *Othello*. Famous last song? Could be, who cares? Do you? Neither do I.

Andiamo, she sings and I get into my lonely bed, too tired to undress. My last thoughts are about the willow tree Desdemona muses about, and I wonder sleepily what is going to become of my splendid weeping willow given the raging storm. And what about all the animals in the unrelenting fury outside?

FALL

I wake up in one piece and in my clothes, having slept like all the many scattered logs I can see from my bed, since I didn't bother—too tipsy, I presume—to close the shutters last night, refusing to exclude the raging storm. I still have electricity. The radio-clock glows red on the nightstand. I turn on the radio. Reports are devastating. The ferocious lady left her fingerprints on few states; shamelessly ravaged those on her way, before taking her mad spree on to the north.

I stumble out of bed, submitting to Rita's complaints. I appease her with some of yester-night's remains and start a strong espresso. While it gurgles I look at the huge weeping willow between the barn and the farmhouse. It has suffered some damage, but is still standing tall though stooping. Looking at it, I realize fall has come, I can feel autumn in my bones. I shudder, not unpleasantly. Here comes my season.

I let Rita out. She is adjusting to her new surroundings, and if her needs are urgent she leaves our safe abode alone.

I see something moving on the grass and assume it's a big groundhog. I am relieved to see it and hope all the other members of my private National Geographic's Zoo are safe. The poor animal seems to turn in circles; probably another one of the many victims the savage beauty left behind her.

Defeated, I accept my decreasing eyesight and turn to the binoculars. What a strange groundhog, all furry and what lovely spectacles around its eyes. Oh no, it is a raccoon! My first close-up of a raccoon turning in circles. Where did I hear about it? Recollecting I am already rushing with all my might toward unsuspecting Rita, screaming her name. A nocturnal raccoon out in daylight is dangerous, said Lea, chances are it has rabies. Rita, about to befriend the newcomer, sniffing around it for its consent, turns to me wagging her tail. A second time in the last twelve hours I grab her up in my arms and rush breathlessly back home. No more solitary excursions, back to our walks together, far away from the maddening raccoon.

I organize the place, putting away all evidences of my last night's apprehensions: candles, flashlight and the likes. I sit down to read essays by my students, but Rita is serenading her desires. I put on my sneakers, preaching to her about the need to take my wants into consideration as well.

Out we go, not before I check the meadow for the raccoon. The rabies coast is clear and Rita and I are into our ritual stroll down by the river when I see the puddles. Three of them, large ones and getting larger by the second. We do venture to the river's bank and stand there gaping: the stream makes my head spin. Lots of debris floats on the raging water, wood, Styrofoam, leaves, branches, whatnot. So the deluge did not spare us! I rush back home, Rita on my heels, and call Manny.

Despite the urgency I say good morning and how are you and yes I am fine before blurting, "The water is rising!"

"I know," he says nonchalantly.

"But…but what shall I do?"

"Nothing."

"What do you mean nothing? I have to evacuate the basement; there are boxes of photos, books, newspaper scraps, memorabilia."

"The water will not get to the barn."

"But the river is already overflowing!"

"It will not get there; I will come later and check if you are alarmed."

Alarmed! No, I am not alarmed in the least, I will stand here and watch your memories be swept away, your manuscripts, photos, old diaries, extra copies of all your publications. The things I haven't had the heart to unpack. Yet.

I look out at the river rushing with gusto, faster and faster, the puddles have emerged into a big one and the meadow is beginning to look like a lake. I go down to the basement and gaze with despair at all the boxes, too many, and there is no way I can lift any of them on my own. Why didn't I ask the movers to put them up at the ghost wing? Was it out of respect to your privacy, my darling? Stop grinning at my account!

I am at my window seat, trying to convince myself that if the water gets to the basement and maybe higher I will lose everything and be at long last lightweight and free. And if I drown as well, so be it.

Manny arrives; I am trying to look calm. We go out and he examines the shimmering lake.

"No, I don't think it will reach the house. Tell you what; we'll stick a branch here, if the water comes that far, we will evacuate the basement." So we stick a branch and scare away two reptiles rushing for a swim in the new lake.

"Snakes," says Manny indifferently, "they are harmless."

Do they know it? I wonder in silence. Snakes frighten me. I am a city girl, after all.

But I am playing brave. The elements are not going to get to me.

I ask Manny about the projectors. "These are storm lights," he explains, "They turn on when the wind is high."

I tell him about the raccoon, and he advises me not to let Rita out on her own. If it weren't for the floods he would have called the police. They shoot raccoons out of their element. Thank you, Your Majesty Hurricane, for small graces.

He has to go, houses and farms closer to the creek have already been flooded and some have lost power. "Call me if the water reaches the branch," he says and leaves me with the impending deluge, huddled in my window seat, watching the water get closer and closer, thinking about Emperor Nero, who played his harp and sang while watching Rome burn. I heard you; you said it is a myth, okay, but so is a large portion of human history, as you said time and again. Are you having fun yet, exempt of earthly worries such as I am going through?

I am not going to drown in self-pity imagining how romantic all this could have been with you around. You weren't the greatest romantic ever, not with me, but still, it is a kind of adventure for two, as Noah knew.

The lake comes closer and I decide to stop looking at it hypnotized and do something productive. My desk is just above my private lake and I could have enjoyed the delightful scene much more if I weren't scared.

I go out trying to ignore the snakes. The water is starting to lick the branch we planted. I am about to call Manny when his pickup truck pulls up and he comes out walking toward me slower than ever. He stands by my side on the lake's board, watching the mounting water. A man and a woman under Pennsylvania's blushing sky, in front of a pretty lake, what's wrong with that picture?

"This is it," he says finally, "the water is not going to come farther."

"How do you know?"

"The people who built back then knew what they were doing, look how high the barn sits. You have nothing to worry about." His cell phone rings; yes, he is coming at once, he promises, and rushes over to more hazardous cases. And here I am, alone again, facing my private deluge and trying to keep calm about it.

Back in the basement contemplating the boxes, debating which one should be saved, I open the first at hand and of all things find a photo album, yours and Amanda's. I sit on the carpeted floor and look compulsively at the mostly black-and-white pictures. You seem in love, glowing, smiling, holding hands, hiking, skiing, honeymooning in Europe. In other pictures, you two are beaming proudly with rotund baby-Benjamin.

What went wrong? Maybe it was your decision to move back to Israel? But by then you were divorced. Or is it that Amanda had enough of your arrogance, you were both too competitive for each other, but who knows, besides you, wherever you are, and maybe her, and I will probably never find out and you are right, it is none of my business. It is part of never understanding why you chose me, unless it was your need to be with the exact opposite of Amanda.

And it hurts today as it hurt years ago, when I was so intoxicated with you and listened with starry eyes to your Amanda's accolades. For a long time I reassured myself by saying, "Amanda is the past, I am the present," but her past presence was quite emphasized in our shared lives and strangely enough is still felt despite your death. I wish I knew where all those tears come from and how is it they never have time to dry. I was never a great crier till your premature explosive departure. Mourning becomes Daphne. Only it doesn't. I wish I could get over you, Alon, but it seems as if it is not about to happen.

So what if the water continues to mount and eventually flood the basement, my tears are helping and I can just picture Alice's drowning in her own tears in Wonderland. It could be an ideal way to drown my—our—past once and for all. It might eliminate the souvenirs if not the memories. Enough of gloomy thoughts, Rita and I are taking a stroll to the banks of the silver lake, reflecting the evening clouds floating slowly in the sky. It seems as if the water is still; maybe Manny was right and the lake is not going to invade the barn. I am almost sorry; I was beginning to like the idea of drowning my past sorrows.

*

A few leaves have been falling at leisure all summer long, imitating the slow-floating snowflakes supposed to come later, but they were not predicting fall. Still, fall is here and not only because fall semester started some weeks ago. It is here because the wind is colder, the evenings balmy and sometimes chilly and the corn is being harvested. Not the cornfields around the barn, they are for feed and will have to wait longer. And it is a perfect time to give in to Nell's insistence and Dea's gentle invitation and take the bus to The

Big City. New York is less than two hours away and still I look at it as a major journey. Everything seems major since you left—that is how I am trying to think lately about your departure—compared to the huge changes I made, when all I wanted to do was to be burned, okay, just buried by your side.

I have to pull myself by my bootstraps in order to get going. I need weekends to recuperate, to fill up my batteries, to finish unfinished business, if that's humanly possible. Mainly I need time to be free and daydream at my window seat without rushing around.

But I was out of excuses, and here I am sitting on a bus without being paralyzed by fear of bombs. To some degree the suicide bombers in my Middle East made bus riders into their main target and thus established a horrible separation in status between those who can afford a car and those who can't. So many new immigrants and foreign workers lost their lives for a conflict they had no part in. Older people on their way to the market, kids on their way to school. But of course there are more and more exceptions. Like you, my love, blown into pieces in a coffee shop, and others at malls, restaurants, hotels and cafeterias.

I guess I was reluctant to go to NYC because it reminds me of you, but then everything does. You took me there for my first time and proudly showed me "your" city. I was so impressed by it all, you, the city. I followed you awed and admiring, feeling small, inadequate and lost. Provincial.

Manhattan's skyline always excites me, and I feel the ghost-presence of the fallen Twin Towers. Hazy and tempting, shimmering chimera. Sin City you called her lovingly. The city where you met, fell in love, and lived with Amanda. Not to mention married and fathered a child. Why does it still hurt after your death? Maybe because I never felt you were really mine, although legally you were. As if legal really matters, maybe it does once you are widow. I was the official widow during your funeral and later on, and all the others, admiring female students and colleagues, were not. They came home to express condolences although oftentimes I felt they needed the consolation. I provided as best as I could.

Stepping down the bus, I feel lost. I have the restaurant's address and can still hail a cab, but I stand dazzled by sound and fury, I have lived too long like a hermit in my peaceful barn. I am shoved and pushed and forced to move on, finally standing in a long line waiting for my cab. The couple ahead of me is Israeli. It seems natural to me at first, and then I realize I am in NYC and it seems, again, appropriate, no less than the Japanese-speaking young women behind me. The man says something in Hebrew about getting ahead of the line and the woman talks him out of it. I hear you commenting nastily about the Israeli rudeness, but then, Alon my darling, you were part of it. Bluntness was no stranger to you, and you did work your way through without too many scruples. But you were judgmental as they come; often criticizing others for faults you had in abundance. No, I am not maintaining a feud with you; it is just my way of coping, cultivating posthumous anger, almost never felt or recognized while you were still around. Why was I so oblivious to your faults when you were here? I don't think it has anything to do with love being blind. I saw your numerous shortcomings but accepted them with indulgence. Death should be blinder but it seems like an eye opener. In a way I wish I could go on living in denial, adoring you the way I did, but I suppose I am into the anger stage, will I ever get to the forgive and forget one? Probably not in this lifetime.

The Israeli couple keeps turning around and staring rudely while whispering excitedly to each other. Can they guess I understand their language?

Finally the woman turns around and says in Hebrew, "I know you."

"You do?" I say, taken aback.

The man turns around and says, "You were on television!"

"I don't think so," I say, embarrassed.

"Yes, yes, something to do…" She stops and puts her hand to her mouth. "A…"

Her husband whispers in her ear something I can't hear. They both look at me with pity. It is their turn to take a cab. The woman says, "You take it."

"You were ahead of me," I say.

"No, no, go ahead."

I can feel the people behind me getting agitated so I step into the cab feeling awkward and before I slam the door I hear the woman say, "Poor thing."

What does it mean? How do they know? What do they know? Unlike you, I was never on television, never had my photo in a newspaper. I never went public about your death. The media did its usual and even more, and interviewed whoever they could lay their microphones and cameras on, but not me, never me. And out of the blue, treacherous tears are swelling in my throat. I give the driver the restaurant's address in a shaky voice, thinking about the couple, about Israelis in general: one moment they were thinking of ways to cut the line and then, recognizing me as one of theirs, worse, an unfortunate victim of a hostility act, they generously gave me their place. How typical. I am touched. The tears. Who am I kidding? I feel sorry for myself and I wish I didn't.

The city is divulging itself: soaring, noisy, hectic and magnificent. Such a contrast to my peaceful barn, and still I can appreciate its urban beauty. The colors and diversity, the crazy heartbeat of the city help me swallow back my tears. Your ghost roams the large avenues lit by stray sun rays sneaking beyond the clouds; how you loved this city! How much like you she seems to me: arrogant, vain, dazzling, charismatic, misleading. Where did that word come from all of a sudden? Or maybe it is not so sudden. I feel betrayed, I am betrayed, your death betrayed me, darling, the ultimate betrayal. And maybe you betrayed me while you were still alive. I don't mean with other women, because I knew you couldn't resist temptation; no, the betrayal has to do with my blindness to your faults, my refusal to see you for who you were. No, it's not your fault, it is mine. It was my choice.

Why am I allowing such thoughts to spoil this lovely autumn day in New York?

Sirens are part of the city's soundtrack, but here I am not afraid, not constantly scared of another bomb. Although this city has had her share of terror.

The driver asks, "Which side?"

"Which side?" I repeat, puzzled.

"East or west?"

"I don't know... Are we there?" I fumble in my purse for change. I pay and get out confused. I don't see the restaurant. I turn to ask the cab driver but he already has a new costumer. I stand there on the pavement lost and stupid and the tears are again tricking their way up my throat. I look at the restaurant's address, hating you for not being here for me when I need you. Hating myself even more for being so childish and helpless. I take a deep breath, some steps forward and I see the restaurant. I feel an overwhelming relief, still angry with myself. *"You tend to switch the anger onto yourself,"* I hear the trauma therapist. I venture into the restaurant, chin up.

Nell is immediately all over me, smelling and looking gorgeous as always. Of all my friends she is the most outgoing, outspoken, confident and lovely, my total opposite and still we have been friends since the first time Alon introduced us to each other. She became my friend and sort of older mentor, by far more seasoned than I will ever be. She hugs me and then looks at me with her critical eye.

"I have seen you look better," she says.

"Under the circumstances," I say.

"And worse, you looked by far worse last time we met."

Last time we met was during the *shiva* after Alon's death. She flew over to Israel just to be there with me.

She leads the way to the table she chose, the best; Nell always gets what she wants.

She sits by my side, holding my arm. I don't have to look around in order to know every man in sight would love to be in my place. Still, I detect a few new lines under her eyes, but they just add to her attractiveness.

I realize we talk in English. Nell now lives most of the time in NYC with Al, her rich new husband, who adores her. No denying NYC becomes her.

She orders champagne. I try to protest and give up. I am not going to spoil the party and a party it is, whenever we meet, even amidst big crises and dire straits.

"You haven't been to my barn," I accuse her.

"I will eventually."

We order huge sandwiches to go with the champagne and I already feel much better. We eat and drink and laugh, Nell tells me about the art gallery she is about to open in a loft, not far away. She intends to take me there after lunch. I laugh out loud the way one does with Nell, with or without champagne. It has been awhile since I heard my laugher and I like the sound.

We leave the restaurant arm in arm and I feel proud the way I always feel around Nell. The same I felt around Alon. The way I feel in the company of beautiful people as if their loveliness is projected on me.

Next thing Nell is pushing me into a little store and I think it might be the gallery just to realize—blushing and wishing I was not—we are in a sex store.

"What—" I start, but Nell puts her finger to her mouth.

"Look at this!" She marvels at what seems like a pocket vibrator.

I look around us, there are other customers and everyone seems to mind their own business. "I thought you said Al is a great lover," I whisper in her ear.

"He is—so what? Everybody can use some enhancing, even you! Look at this; I think I will buy it for you."

"Nell!"

"What? Don't tell me sex died with Alon!"

The treacherous tears. She looks at me, grabs my hand. "Sorry, Daphne. I just don't want you to mourn forever."

I nod, not trusting my voice.

"Don't you feel the urge?" she asks, incredulous.

I shrug. "Not too often…"

"I know you were crazy for Alon, but I am not sure he made you happy. Sexually."

I am dumbfounded.

"He was too self-centered," she says, and puts on the counter a strange devise. "I am buying it for you and you do with it whatever you want. Throw it out when you find a lover or use it with him."

A lover.

"I know it is too early but you are young and attractive and I don't believe you are going to be on your own for long. I know; I know, you are still in love with Alon, but this will fade. The way it happened to me."

Nell lost her husband during the 1973 war, she was pregnant with their son.

I don't think I can fathom myself with anybody else, with any body, including the mini-vibrator, but I take the little wrapped parcel she hands me, toss it carefully in my purse and say, "Thank you."

The art gallery is beautiful. But then everything Nell touches becomes stunning. There are only four paintings hanging on the walls, large paintings that seem to furnish and fill the whole space. I stand in front of each painting and feel again the tears climbing, but this time they express excitement and bliss. I stare at the pictures, one after the other, savoring their beauty, their magnificent transparence. They are alike and yet very different, colorful and illuminated, each reflecting a different mood, maybe a different season. They are simple yet complex, they look familiar although I know I never saw them before. Maybe they depict an intimate landscape, the artist's, mine, or both. They do not require analyzing, just admiration.

"Amazing, aren't they?" says Nell.

I nod.

"You should meet the artist," she says.

"Hello, girls." Al is here, jolly as always. He kisses my cheek and embraces Nell. "So what have you been up to?" he asks.

"Sex store," replies Nell.

"Oh?" he says, pulling a Groucho Marx face.

Nell laughs gaily.

I glance at my watch. "I have to be at Dea's," I say.

They both escort me out and insist I take a cab. "It is rush hour," I protest, heading to the subway, but Al has already hailed a cab and in I go, as they stand and wave at me.

Dusk is descending on the city and I think about twilight in my barn and feel for the first time homesick. I guess it is home now.

*

The trees keep changing their colors and I don't know if there are enough words in English, or in any other language, to describe the tones and hues of the different shades, the new daily transformations of forms and textures. Rita and I take our daily walk; the forest is becoming more and more accessible as the leaves drift slowly downward, gently waltzing, dotting the ground with a rusty orange-brown-red crackling carpet. It is the sensual dance of the seven vibrant veils stripping at leisure to nakedness. Some of the leaves went fast with the strong wind we had whistling its winter tune.

Behind the trees Rita and I discover a little pond that was not accessible till now. The river turns and creates a small delta. We watch two idle ducks swim at leisure till we interrupt the silence. Rita is frightened by the rattle of their wings when they take off in protest. I look awed at the beauty around me. The acute feeling that all this is temporary—for me—makes it even more astonishing. The trees stand majestically unaware of their splendor, the river flows away full of yesterday's rain. The grass is greener than green, and some deer still wander around late in the afternoon. One was on the road when I drove to college this morning and was there again—or still—when I came back. It looked at me—at the car—mesmerized, and only when I got really close it sprung and ran away into what remains of the forest. No place to hide anymore as the forest is diminishing; the deer are becoming darker and darker, preparing to blend with the graying landscape. Is it possible that Rita is changing her color as well? She seems darker!

I saw pickup trucks coming down our private driveway and asked Manny about them. He said the hunting season has begun and that at first the hunters are allowed to use only bows and arrows. It is so much crueler. I picture Frieda Kalo's painting of herself as a gazelle whose flesh is torn by arrows.

The phone is ringing when I get home and I answer out of breath.

Dad's anxious voice: "Daphne?"

"Is something wrong?"

"No, no. Are you okay?"

"Yes, under the circumstances," I say and smile to myself, *I sound like you, Dad.*

"Happy New Year."

"Sorry?"

And then it dawns on me. It is Rosh Hashanah, the Jewish New Year's Eve.

"Oh, Dad, I forgot all about it."

"Well, yes."

"So what are you doing tonight?"

"I don't know. Actually a friend invited me over."

"Someone I know?"

"I guess…yes."

Silence.

"Who?" I probe.

"Erica."

"Erica?"

"Erica."

"Alon's mother?"

"Yes." Obviously he doesn't want to talk about it. But my curiosity is burning.

"So is it going to be a big celebration?"

"I don't think so. It is too soon, you know."

I say nothing. Too soon after Alon's death, or maybe too soon in this strange relationship. It is weird. Almost incestuous. Imagine, Alon, your mom and my dad.

"Do you see each other often?" I ask quickly before I have time to think about it. I can hear him hesitating.

"She lives close by," he says and I can feel he doesn't want to talk about it.

And why not, Alon, they do have a lot in common besides being related to each other through our marriage. But it would have never crossed my mind. Or yours for that matter, you were quite possessive about your mother. About all women in your life, come to think about it.

"So you didn't know it is New Year's Eve," Dad says to change the subject.

"No."

"But you do remember Yom Kippur is in ten days."

"No, I don't," I say, "Actually I think I am teaching that day."

"You are teaching on Yom Kippur?!" he exclaims, incredulous.

"Why not?"

"Daphne!"

"Dad, since when do you care about religious days?"

"Yom Kippur is not just a religious day."

"You never fasted on Yom Kippur."

"No, but I never worked either. Except."

And we both know what the "except" stands for. Except in the camps.

There is nothing I can say.

"You will cancel, right?"

"How can I cancel? I have thirty students in my class."

"So?"

"Dad, you always said dates were of no importance. It is just a meaningless date."

"Not for Jews, it is not."

"Dad!"

"Are you teaching tomorrow?"

"Yes."

"It is New Year's Day!"

"Dad you are not turning into a born-again Jew, are you?"

"I don't have to be born again. I was born and still am a Jew."

"Me too, but I don't have to cancel classes because of that. I don't understand you; you were always so…secular."

"It is not the same thing when you live abroad!"

"Why should it be different?"

"Daphne, you know pretty well why. Please cancel your classes."

All of a sudden I feel like the kid I was more than thirty years ago. Begging to stay at a friend's house for the night. He was so protective. As if something terrible is about to happen any moment.

I do understand where it stems from, still, this Yom Kippur thing is different and I am an adult now.

"Dad, you always respected my beliefs, right?"

"Right, but I find it difficult to respect your disbeliefs, especially since you are living in the Gola." I never heard him use that word before. He will say "abroad," but never "Gola," which is Diaspora in Hebrew. A word loaded with meaning.

"I have to go," he says, "Promise me you will cancel."

"I will think about it. Give Erica my regards."

"I will. Happy New Year."

"Happy New Year."

I sit at my window seat, looking outside blind to the fall's beauty. Too many changes. Dad and Erica. Dad caring about my teaching on Kippur. And the fact that I completely forgot about the Jewish New Year.

I figure I might as well go through one ceremony I always kept, eating an apple with honey to ensure a sweet year. Although I am sure we both dipped an apple in honey a year ago and look how bitter this year was, or is yours sweet wherever you are?

So I will skip this superstition as well as canceling teaching on Yom Kippur. I reflected upon it briefly when I was preparing my syllabus. It has no meaning for me and now, after your death, less than ever, so why fuss about it? And how come Dad cares? He used to claim no God would have allowed the Holocaust.

He is changing. He is old, but he sounded lucid. He is lucid. He still has his bright scientific mind. So what is going on? The only explanation I can think of is that he still can't come to terms with the fact I chose, for the moment, to live outside of Israel. This is something I can understand. As far as he is concerned once the State of Israel was created it became the only place where Jews can and should live. And I know Erica thinks the same way. I hear you laughing, Alon, my cynic beyond death, but I don't find it funny. I understand both our—remaining—parents, but I will stand my ground. I pour myself a glass of chilled white wine, it was a hot day, and I toast the living and the dead, and ask whoever is in charge, if there is anyone, for a better year, knowing it will take no less than a miracle.

*

It is the eve of Yom Kippur, I call Dad before Yom Kippur starts and I can't lie to him when he asks if I intend to teach tomorrow. He sent me an express letter detailing why he thinks I shouldn't teach on Yom Kippur. I read and reread his letter, crying a bit since he elaborated on the *price we paid and still are paying for being Jews*.

I tell him on the phone that it is going to be a special class, since I am going to discuss "Shema," the bloodcurdling poem Primo Levi wrote upon his return from Auschwitz.

"There is no connection whatsoever," he says.

"Oh no? So how come you insist on my canceling the classes?"

"Yom Kippur has nothing to do with the Holocaust."

"Are you positive?"

He doesn't answer and then says, so typical of him: "The English version of the poem is not as good as the Italian or even the Hebrew translation."

"I don't know about the Italian, but yes, you are right, it sounds better in Hebrew since Levi paraphrases on the original *Shema* prayer."

I know he is angry with me, but I am determined. Yom Kippur is when God is supposed to decide who lives and who dies. After what I have been through this last year, who cares? Live or die, you took such a substantial part of me when you died, what do I have to lose?

Yes, I know, I look out there and the splendor is overwhelming. The fall dresses the rusting trees in all shades of gold, orange, red, especially now, when the setting sun makes everything glow. I admit it makes living worthwhile. Although there is the guilt. Well, Yom Kippur is when guilt is legitimate; it is the grand moment of the Jewish Mea Culpa. The soul-searching day. I think I remember how we "celebrated" it a year ago. The way we always did. You felt compelled to break the rules, therefore the day of fasting and chest beating was for you the day of pigging out. In every sense. That was your way of challenging your father before and after he died.

And you did have some understandable reasons to be so adamant about Kippur. You lost some of your best friends—and part of your hearing in the left ear—during the horrible Yom Kippur War.

Maybe I am doing the same to my dad. I am only beginning to grasp how thoroughly I was influenced by you, how often I imitated you, consciously and unconsciously. Will I ever let go? Would you ever let go of me? No, I don't want you to go. I already lost you for real. Let your sometimes tormenting spirit live on in me. Through me till I die.

So if someone is watching me sip my wine by the window, yes, please, take me away to join my one and only dead love.

*

I have no regrets on my way to college. Certainly not while swimming through the mass of rusty rustling leaves covering my path. I encounter some hunters out for the deer and think about their God, the deer's and the hunters', deciding who shall live and who shall die. No lightning strikes me while I drive peacefully, up and down the soft hills of Pennsylvania, Kippur or not Kippur.

The students are there as usual, on time and waiting for me silently. So unlike the untamed students back in Israel, who arrive late ("The Traffic"), and talk among themselves incessantly.

I ask my students, "Does anyone know what day is today?"

"Monday?" some say hesitantly.

They are uncertain, all the time, all of them. It is typical Pennsylvania Dutch, explained Karen. Most will not participate, especially the freshmen.

"Does anybody know what Yom Kippur is?"

Michael raises his hand tentatively.

"Yes?"

"I think it is a Jewish holiday when you are supposed to fast?"

"Correct." I explain briefly about death, life and atonement, the meaning of *Kippur*, atonement in Hebrew. Then I give them each a copy of the poem and ask them to read and then comment. They read and they don't comment so I ask some to tell the class how the poem affects them.

"Well," says Robin reluctantly, "it is what you always tell us, not to take things for granted," and he reads: "*You who live safe / in your warm houses, / you who find, returning in the evening ,/ hot food and friendly faces*… We should be thankful for what we have, I think."

"Yes, by all means you should, but this is not what the poem is all about. Tammy, what do you think?"

"He curses us," she says indignantly.

"How do you mean?"

"He writes: *Repeat them to your children, / Or may your house fall apart, / May illness impede you, / May your children turn their faces from you.*"

So now I have to explain Levi's meaning, and hearing myself justifying the passing on of Holocaust memories from generation to generation I understand Dad better and feel remorse.

Yes, Father is right, Primo Levi was right, those who were there have to keep telling it again and again. But in my head I still argue with Dad, saying, teaching in Kippur did grant me the opportunity to let my students read "Shema." Is it going to linger in their minds? Who knows, but this is one question no teacher should ask.

Karen is waiting for me after class. "Do you have a moment for some tea?"

"Absolutely."

We walk to the students' cafeteria and stand in line for a cup of tea. I tell Karen about my version of Yom Kippur; she laughs and relates her own revolt against her God.

"At first, when my husband, ex-husband, got drunk and beat me, I used to pray. But then with time I realized nobody was listening or helping. I was bruised inside out and it went on and on with no heavenly interference whatsoever."

She pauses; I sip my tea and nibble on a cookie, no heavenly intervention on account of that terrible sin committed on Yom Kippur.

"What happened then?"

"He started beating the kids. So I divorced him and my church."

"Do you miss him?"

"My hubby or God?"

"Both."

"Not in the least," she says and we laugh merrily.

Driving home, I think how deceiving is the magnificence of this place. Haven for me right now, yes, but no real paradise on this earth; everyone has a share of misery, no matter where they live. But then, stopping at the supermarket and going in without having to open my handbag for security inspection, without thinking, *This could be my last moment on earth,* I tell myself there are some major advantages living here, at least for me, at least now.

*

The landscape is becoming considerably naked. The other side of the river is exposed now, and all of a sudden I am less isolated, I can see some glimmering lights in the distance and the distance is not as dramatic as when the leaves were there to hide and shield me.

The deer are darker and darker and fewer and fewer, I fear; the hunters are still around, and now the real hunting season has started. I am told it is better that way because otherwise the deer will eat all the green. The bucks are now coming forth, scared as they are, probably coaxed by hunger. One of them marked the tree against my living room's window. I don't mind sharing it with him.

The cornfields all around were harvested, but not the one next to the barn. It is turning slowly yellow and dry and shrinking a bit. The gusting wind is sending the long leaves flying all over the meadow. We had our premature frost already and even this morning, the pastures were white and frosty and splendid and gave the first impressions of how they are going to look in a short while, when winter spreads its white freezing cloak.

I have a brief fall break and am indulging in welcoming the fall soon to turn into winter, putting away my summer clothes, trying some new, warmer outfits. I have two sets of attire, those you saw and those you didn't. Not that you really saw what I had on, most of the time you looked right through me. When you had a foul mood you used to make nasty comments about my bad taste. I will not fight with you, Alon darling, I wish you were here so that we could cuddle together; it is getting colder, and I already had my oil delivery to suffice, they said, till springtime. I even bought my share of wood and am about to start the gorgeous fireplace in the living room. I don't really know how to do it. There must be a certain order, I guess I will just put some logs, papers and throw in a match.

It is lonely without you, fireplaces are meant for two. The days are getting shorter and the nights longer. Dark falls at once now, like a black veil covering the shedding forest in silence.

The phone rings, it is a surprising hour since it's nighttime in Israel. It could be Dea or Nella.

"Daphne?" Unfamiliar voice but the Israeli accent is soothing.

"Yes?"

"It is Dan. Dan Sahar."

"Oh, hello." I switch to Hebrew, my voice warming.

"How are you?"

"Fine. Fine, actually I am not very far from you."

"You are?" How on earth did he get my phone number or address? Lots of possibilities: Edna, Ram, someone at the faculty in Jerusalem.

"I think so. I am halfway from Philadelphia, I have to give a lecture tomorrow at Penn…I thought…"

I know what's coming and freeze.

"I thought we might have a drink together, or dinner, if you have time."

I am dying to say no, but can't bring myself to say it. You were friends. Friends and rivals, at least academically.

"Well…"

"I could come over and pick you up."

"It is not so easy to find."

"Oh," he laughs, "I was a navigator in the army."

How very typical, the famous Israeli arrogance.

"What's your exact address?"

I give it to him, too embarrassed to say, *Sorry, I am busy*. I was looking forward to my dinner alone, at my window seat, music, wine, first fire. Reminiscing about you. But I can hear you, *Be more social, for heaven's sake,* something you told me quite often.

"I will be there in no time," says Dan and hangs up.

I stay there with the dead phone in my hand feeling angry and mainly stupid. Why didn't I say NO?

I go back to sorting my clothes but then realize I have to change. He said something about going out. I try one outfit and then another. I look at the mirror and dislike the severe woman sternly looking back at me. I wind up putting on some garments you never saw, a pair of corduroy pants and a new sweater, in off white.

Reluctantly I put on some makeup. I am growing used to my solitude and liking it more and more. I hardly know this person, why on earth would he want to see me? Well, maybe he wants to talk about you, and this is always welcome, but still, I am less than thrilled. I vaguely remember him coming to your funeral and to your *shiva*.

You never liked him as far as I can recall, but you spent some time together, debating about war and peace, negotiations, and the eternal dilemma: is there someone—on the other camp—to talk to. You, my love, were always for peace, for negotiations, for talking with whoever is willing to talk. Dan, if I remember correctly, believed that the only way to peace is by intimidation, by showing our strength, because "this is the only language they understand." "They" the Arabs in general, Palestinians in particular. You and Dan disliked each other but made a great team on television panels and on different campuses around the world.

I am expecting the phone to ring and Dan's embarrassed voice asking for directions, the way everybody else does, including furniture deliverers from the area, phone and computer installers, except my—our—Dea, who arrived without a hitch.

Sure enough, the doorbell rings, and I rush to open the door with dismay. Rita is barking for her life, she always does when the doorbell rings.

"God," says Dan, "why on earth would anyone in her right mind choose to live in such a remote place?"

"Come in," but he is already inside, and I am not surprised at his bluntness and lack of any greeting. Right, I have been here for several months but not enough time to forget the Israeli straightforwardness. Now it feels like sandpaper on my new sensitivity from being with people around here: always polite, discreet and gentle. Bluntness I do not miss.

He doesn't look around. Most people who step in always look with awe and admiration at the striking, huge space, the old dark beams.

"I told you I could find the place real easy," he says, huffing and puffing as if he walked all the way.

I lead him to the living room, not expecting any compliments on the gorgeous fireplace, where the fire is dancing gaily, or about my new accommodating furniture. He does accommodate himself, in front of the fireplace, still out of breath, is he excited or is it just his weight?

"What would you like to drink?" I ask, being my new Pennsylvania Dutch. Or is it the way I grew up? After all, both my parents are the Jewish version of the local Dutch, German Jews.

"What do you have?"

"Orange juice, soda, water, wine?"

"Wine will do. What kind of wine do you have?"

"Only red."

"Fine."

In the kitchen I pour him a glass of wine and come back. He has caught his breath. I hand him the wine.

"Aren't you joining me?"

I don't know what to say so I just go back to the kitchen and pour myself a glass.

"To us," he toasts, grinning.

I sit as far away as I can, and raise my glass silently, saying nothing.

"So," he says cheerfully, "how is your new life?"

"Well…I…"

"You run away from it all, right?" and he laughs.

I say nothing.

He sips his wine and looks around. "Nice place you have got yourself."

"We got it together," I say, "Alon and me."

"How much do you pay for it?" he asks.

And although it is such a typical Israeli question, I am shocked, I forgot, got used to my new way of life, to different behaviors. I just say, "Enough, but I can afford it, you know, I work here."

"Good," he says and repeats mechanically, "Good, good."

I sip my wine. What now?

He gets up, stands by the fire, pokes it, and puts on a fresh log, feeling utterly at home.

Rita the traitor walks to him and stands there, waiting for him to caress her. He ignores her so she comes to me for consolation. I caress her behind her ears the way she likes.

"Aren't you afraid to live alone in the middle of nowhere?"

"Why should I be?"

"I don't know, you can be murdered, raped… This is America, not Israel."

"That is the whole point," I say, "I have no fear here."

"Good," he says again, "good, good."

I know it is mechanical. Why does it exasperate me?

"I can imagine how hard it was, is still…" he says and I am more taken aback by his sympathy than I was by his directness.

I am looking for words, but he goes on, "I know because I am going through the same ordeal as yours."

I am thinking fast, as far as I know his wife is safe and sound and so are his children. Like every Israeli in and out of the country I obsessively read the names of the dead in any bomb explosion.

"Ruth is fine," he says as if reading my mind, "and the kids as well. No, this is…it is a person very close to me. Was. Still is. I will tell you all about her."

I am not sure I want to hear it, but he goes on, not before sprawling in his seat and gulping down the rest of his wine.

"Ella Rose. She was my translator and editor."

Of course, I knew her vaguely, met her several times, on different occasions, I don't remember ever talking to her, but I suppose we were introduced. I followed her story like everybody else. I can even picture her, curly hair, shy smile, heavy British accent.

He shifts in his place with discomfort, gets up, stands again in front of the fire, goes back and sits down, closer to me, this time. It is my turn to shift uncomfortably in my seat.

"I met her when I was looking for a translator for my first book about Rabin's assassination. I knew of her, but never worked with her. I saw her work and was impressed. I think Alon worked with her, right?"

"No. I don't think so."

"She did mention him, I am positive. Anyway, I remember our first meeting in a little coffee place in Jerusalem. She was very timid. She sat there and listened. She had the most beautiful eyes. When I asked her how much she charged for translation she blushed and said she didn't know, she would have to translate a chapter before she could give me an estimate. I was impressed. I was used to translators charging an arm and a leg. So I said fine, gave her the book and my card, and waited. It didn't take her too long; although I knew she was quite in demand and working for different writers and researchers. The translation was very good, although I needed it for the American public and she was very British. I asked her if she had figured out how much it was going to cost me and she blushed and gave me a sum that was by far less than what I expected. I sat there watching her, trying to digest, and she asked, 'Is it too much?' And I said, 'No, no, it is fine.'"

He stops and picks up his empty wineglass and puts it back and I have to ask, "Would you like some more?"

And he says, "Yes, please."

I go into the kitchen with his glass, refill it and come back. I realize he doesn't want to go out and I am quite hungry. He goes on with his story before I even sit down.

"She did a terrific job. It was sometimes better than the Hebrew version," he says and giggles, as if he doesn't really believe it is possible.

I am fascinated although I know what is coming.

"We spent lots of hours together in her little apartment. We were Americanizing her translation. She was a very lonely woman, did you know?"

I say quietly, "No," but he goes on without hearing me.

"And before long we became lovers. She was very…full of inhibitions. But I think she liked me. She had no expectations, never made demands, was always there for me."

He goes on, not looking at me, gazing at the blazing fire as if seeing her there.

"I was busy. I had my books, my research, my family. I traveled a lot, but she was there whenever I called her. She now translated all my work, edited, advised, and never let me pay her. It was pride, I think; I have never seen anything like it. I know I should have insisted, she was quite broke, you know? But I only found out much later. I guess I took her for granted."

I am impressed by his insight, and moved by his pain.

"Now that I think about her, and I think about her a lot." He stops, finishes his second glass of wine, watches the fire and says, "The truth is I can't stop thinking about her. I realize I know nothing about her. Nothing much. I read lots of stuff afterwards, but at the time I had no idea. She had a large family in Liverpool but she didn't keep in touch. I guess she was that kind of person, rather out of touch. Oh, she knew a lot about me. Always asked about the kids, my work, my meetings. And I spoke constantly, didn't stop to listen. And she was so silent and withdrawn." His voice breaks, I take his glass and mine and go into the kitchen for refills. I cut some cheese, cold cuts and vegetables, and arrange it all on a tray with crackers and olives, giving him some time to compose himself while preparing some things to soothe my hunger and probably his.

I put everything on the little table; he is busy tending the fire.

I sit down and eat some cheese, he joins me, sips his wine and eats, watching the fire.

"When it happened…" His voice breaks, or maybe it is a piece of cheese. "I was not too far, you know? I had no idea. I heard it and then about it, but thought nothing of it. I mean, nothing out of the ordinary.

Or is it ordinary? I was at home, watching television, like we always do when this happens... Nobody called me, I don't think many people knew about our connection. Other than the professional connection, I mean. My wife said, 'I think they are talking about Ella Rose, your translator.' I was shocked. I left the room, went into my study and called her. She didn't have a cell phone. I called her home and got her answering machine time and again. I think I even left a message. I went back to the living room, the television was still on, people were talking about the identified victims and I still refused to believe. Did you feel the same way?" he asks all of a sudden, looking at me.

He doesn't wait for an answer. "I sat there like a zombie, stunned. Hoping it was just a bad dream, waiting to wake up."

"I know the feeling," I hear myself say. He doesn't hear me, and goes on.

"You see, you were Alon's wife, everybody knew it, but no one really knew about us. You identified his body, attended his funeral, sat *shiva*, but I...I was like a stranger, another one of her many acquaintances and people she worked with. I sat in a state of shock in front of the TV, I couldn't move, and when my wife went to bed I just sat there and cried like a baby. I went to her funeral the day after, and it was very painful for me especially since I felt I could not show the depth of my feelings. Of course everybody else there was devastated, but no one realized what I lost. There was no *shiva* since she had no family in Israel. I did approach her brother after the funeral, told him I worked very closely with Ella, begged him to tell me more about her. He just shrugged and said, 'She left England many years ago; I don't know who she really was.' And it is the same way I feel. I don't know who she really was. I never asked her any questions, I just spoke about my life and she sometimes commented, but we never spoke about her or about the way she felt. And I don't think she knew how I felt about her. I didn't know myself till she blew into tiny pieces."

He sips his wine and nibbles on a cracker with cheese. I say nothing. What is there to say? I guess if she were still alive he would be unaware of her feelings, of her life.

"I miss her terribly. I think about her constantly. I carry her photo everywhere." He pulls out of his pocket a worn-out scrap of newspaper with her photo encircled in black. I look at her shy smile and try to guess what she felt for Dan, why she accepted such a relationship.

All of a sudden I am very weary. His story, my memories, maybe the changing season, the logs in the fireplace smoking lazily. I lean back and hope he will go away. But he just sits there immersed in his sorrow, so I start slowly clearing the table, carrying away the empty glasses, the plates, leftovers. He gets up and follows me into the kitchen. I put the dishes in the sink and when I turn around he grabs me in his arms and presses his lips to mine. I freeze. I am totally unprepared and I push him away, saying, "What are you doing?" He tightens his grip on me, saying, "We have a lot in common." And tries again to kiss me, if pressing ones' lips forcefully to a stranger's lips can be called a kiss.

I push him away and say, "We have nothing in common. I am sorry about your loss, but please go away."

He takes a step backward and looks at me incredulous. "Go? Where can I go in the middle of the night? You cannot throw me out!"

A terrible wave of exhaustion and anger engulfs me. "Okay," I say, "you can sleep in the guestroom, but don't try anything, Dan."

He says nothing and goes out and for one happy moment I think he left, but he comes back with his hand luggage and follows me sulking into the guest bedroom.

I go up to my room, angry at myself for allowing this to happen. I can't fall asleep, something is bugging me and I am trying to find out what it is. I keep thinking about Ella, trying to figure out what was there for her in this relationship. And then I realize, this one-sided relationship between Dan and Ella reminds me of our relationship, Alon. You were no less self-centered than Dan, and I, I was your Ella, your devoted editor, adviser, cook, housekeeper, lover. Were you all that for me? At the moment I am not sure. Turning and tossing, I am no longer angry at Dan or at myself, but at Alon, and this time not because he is not here to comfort me in his arms, but because as much as I want to, I cannot ignore his resemblance to Dan and I can't help imagining him loving me posthumously, if I were the one to die.

*

The combine is here this morning and just started harvesting the cornfield that is all yellow and dry. It saddens me because I saw the field when it was first plowed and sowed and then when the green shoots were growing bigger and taller and then when the ears were stemming. Where will the deer hide? And what will they eat? And how are they going to be protected from the frost?

It is going to feel empty, the way it starts to feel with the naked trees all around. A new and different bare landscape I have to adjust to. I miss the greenery although I suppose it will all come back in springtime, whenever that is, still… Strange, since I love the change of seasons, but I guess winter does represent lack and deprivation, death, to some extent. Death, my darling, has become my intimate companion. And as if I needed a further proof I perceive a small raccoon turning in circles on the meadow, I watch it sadly by now knowing something is very wrong if it ventures out during daylight. I will let it be, the way I did last time. I go on cooking, watching the poor raccoon from time to time.

The doorbell rings, Rita barks, and when I open the door one of the farmers is standing there.

"There is a sick raccoon," he says, "please don't let your dog out without a leash."

"I won't," I promise.

I go on with my preparations in the kitchen, looking every now and then at the raccoon performing its sad dance, when a police car pulls by the house. A policeman gets out of the car and heads to the cornfield. Before I get to the living room window I hear a shot and see the poor raccoon heaving on the line between the cornfield and the prairie and I turn my face from the sight and feel the tears starting their independent trail along my cheeks, and then I hear the second shot.

I continue with my chores, trying to stop the deceitful tears. Dea and Mark, her boyfriend, are on their way. I don't want them to see my teary face. I always felt as if I am embarrassing Dea, as if she is ashamed of me. Ever since she was a little girl. As if I didn't correspond to her idea of a mother. I know she admired, still admires, Amanda. I think she was her role model, the kind of woman she wanted to be and has become. I know she sees Amanda often, they are close and she keeps in touch with Benjamin, her half-brother, your spitting image. I was shocked when I last saw him during our visit here. He looked exactly the way you looked when you first walked into that classroom. Dea doesn't resemble you to that extent, but she was your child. Trying to imitate you since she was a toddler. You were her hero and she was the apple of your eye. It is true you grew apart after she moved to the States, but still you visited her whenever you could, and I am certain she was one of the main reasons you wanted to move back here.

Being her only parent now, I feel guilty. As if somewhere in her heart she would have preferred me to die rather than you. I can't help but feel that if I were the one to explode, the loss would not have been as terrible, that I would have been quickly forgotten. And maybe I am wrong, because I still miss my mother. Her death was an awful blow. I used to talk to her before you died. Something else you didn't know about me. She warned me against you; *He will never be faithful to you,* she said. I remember looking at all your female students during your funeral and the *shiva* and thinking, *At least you can't cheat on me anymore.* Are you surprised, if surprise is anything you can experience wherever you are? Oh, I made it easy for you, never asked questions, pretended not to see or hear, the odd hours you kept, flirting conversations you carried on even when I was within earshot, looks exchanged with women. I ignored them all, telling myself I was the one you came back home to. But deep down I always knew you were going to leave me one day. And indeed you did.

I must stop my gloomy thoughts, and look cheerful before Dea and Mark arrive. We are going to celebrate Thanksgiving tomorrow and although I was willing to go through all the motions, bird included, Karen invited us over and I said yes. It is my first Thanksgiving here and I have a lot to be thankful for. A strange statement coming from a fresh widow, but I am referring to the security, the haven, and the peace I find here. Not being afraid to board a bus and not being constantly aware and alarmed about where the next bomb is going to explode. After your death I felt there was nothing more to fear. But then the fear came back. Here I feel safe, although I would have been far more thankful if you were safely by my side. The smallest joy is always so mixed with sorrow and grief. The therapist said it could go on for many years. I must confess the pain is not as acute, but it comes back with a vengeance when I am least prepared, like right now because of the dead raccoon and watching our amazing daughter get out of the car and show the handsome man beside her the barn, towering above the meadow. You would be so proud of her.

I open the door and Dea, who was so withdrawn, is in my arms, hugging, kissing, smiling happily. Yes, this too has changed since your death. She embraces me much more than she did when you were around.

She introduces Mark, who kisses my cheek and smiles.

"Now I know where Dea takes her beauty from," he says.

"Oh no," I say automatically, the way I always have, "she is totally her father."

But my cheeks are on fire. It has been many years since anyone mentioned me and beauty in the same breath.

I show them to the guestroom, regretting stupidly they are not the first to use it, recalling Dan's unwanted visit, and the apologetic phone call the day after I let him stay over. I thought he only wanted to make sure his wife will not hear about it, but he sounded very sincere and said he was sorry he misbehaved, said his misery is affecting his judgment and asked for my forgiveness.

I arrange the lovely roses, white and red, while Dea shows Mark the barn, including the ghost wing, before they go hand in hand to the creek, Rita following them excited, barking out her pleasure. She must get lonely with only me around. I haven't seen Dea so smitten in a long time. Why do I have the feeling you would have been slightly jealous? Maybe because you were always jealous of her men. Starting with the little boyfriend she brought back from kindergarten. You were very protective, doting and possessive as her father. I believe she chose to live in the States partly because she wanted to get away from you. Yes, maybe from me too, but we were not very close, you monopolized her to a certain degree. As if she was your child, not mine. I don't think you were that close to Benjamin, your firstborn. You didn't see much of him. You sure were a more mature and dedicated dad to Dea. She was very much like you. But Mark could be right; I do see her sometimes when I look at photographs of myself as a young woman.

I prepare some drinks and appetizers in the living room and light the fireplace. We all sit together, Rita cuddled blissfully in Dea's lap.

"Mark asked me whether you get lonely living here all by yourself," says Dea. Mark shifts uncomfortably in his seat.

"Don't worry," I tell him, "we Israelis are very blunt."

"Oh," he says, smiling, "this is an understatement."

"And no, I don't get lonely. This is a great place for soul-searching but mainly for recuperating."

"I can imagine how painful it is for you," says Mark.

"It is," I attempt an unsuccessful smile, "but the beauty around here is an amazing balm." We all look out of the windows at the setting sun, inflaming the trees and the grass.

Dea moves closer to Mark, Rita follows her. Mark is feeding Dea while she in her turn feeds Rita. I usually forbid feeding her, but I say nothing.

"Mark lost his father as well," says Dea. "In a car accident a few years ago."

"I am sorry," I tell Mark.

I don't know what to say, and I look at this handsome couple, and feel sad for both of them.

"My mother remarried," says Mark, "I think it was easier for her. They were about to divorce when he died. And I suppose you don't feel enraged the way you do when one dies the way your…the way Dea's father died."

"I don't know if I am enraged," I say, "are you enraged, Dea?"

"I am sad and I am sorry, but no, I am not enraged, not politically. You did mean politically, right?" she asks Mark.

"Yes. I think I would have been furious."

"It is different for us," says Dea. "We grew up with this conflict. Of course I feel there was, and still is, a lot that could and can be done to end the ongoing war, but I am not angry at the Palestinians and not even at the woman who killed Dad. She was a victim of the circumstances as much as he was."

I look at that adult, even, grown-up woman my daughter has become and my heart stirs. She was so enraged and angry as a teenager, revolting against everything, all the time. I am awed and grateful for her serenity, placidity, and maturity.

Mark hugs her and she cuddles in his arms. I get up before my feelings will show and enter the kitchen. "I will start dinner," I say, hoping my voice is not shaking.

Dea follows me and puts her arms around me. I exercise all the restraint I can muster not to burst and cry like a baby.

"I love you, Mom," she says, hugging me. "I am sorry I don't tell you often enough."

I turn away because the tears are already flowing, but Dea goes on hugging me and says, "I know it hurts, Mom, but you will get over him. I promise you."

I shake my head but dare not talk.

Dea helps me with dinner; Mark sets the table and opens a nice bottle of wine.

"I like him," I tell Dea once I can trust my voice.

"He is special," she says. "I am lucky."

"So is he," I say and manage a real smile.

"You don't mind that he is not Jewish?"

"No, darling, you know I don't care about religion."

"I thought so, but I needed to hear it. We are moving in together."

"What lovely news!" I say and it is my turn to hug my wonderful daughter.

*

It is Thanksgiving afternoon and I take out of the fridge the hummus I prepared. I did it the long and elaborate way, although they sell it ready-made.

"Look at the way we Israelis adopted the Arab cuisine and claim it as our own," Dea tells Mark, sealing the hummus dish.

On our way to Karen's house we get lost. Dea is driving and I am the inapt navigator. I did print out the directions but it seems they weren't accurate. Dea and Mark are starving but they are patient and understanding. Mark takes charge and after turning around in several peaceful neighborhoods, we arrive at Karen's place.

Lots of people are crowded into her house. We are being introduced to a variety of strangers, and everyone is warm and welcoming.

Being a newcomer, I am relieved to realize I am not the only foreigner—or alien, as we are officially called.

Everybody is cheerful; Dea and Mark are engaged in conversation with some of the younger guests. I try to help Karen in the kitchen but she takes me to the living room and sits me on a cozy sofa next to Ron, her young brother. He tells me he too is a college professor and that he teaches chemistry at Princeton. I am impressed, as I always am by people who deal with "real" science. We chat about students. He says his students are by far less shy than the students I describe. "I know what you are talking about," he laughs, "I graduated here and it was no different back then. This is your typical Pennsylvania Dutch, they are quite withdrawn. Why don't you make them write an essay about it?"

"What a marvelous idea, indeed, I will. How come," I ask, some of the good punch already turning my head and freeing my tongue, "you became so open and friendly when you grew up?"

"Ah!" he says, smiling and leaning closer to me. "I moved away! But seriously, I think it has to do with their age. What kind of young woman were you at eighteen?"

"Well, I, like everybody else in my country, was in the army at eighteen. But yes, you are right; I was rather shy when I was a young student."

"As if you are not nowadays as well," says Karen, joining our conversation.

"Is she?" asks Ron, looking at his sister.

"She is," affirms Karen.

"So she came to the right place, Pennsylvania is perfect for her!"

"It is," I say, "I love it here. My father is sort of Pennsylvania Dutch: conservative and very German."

"It's time to eat," announces Karen, and she leads us to the long table full of goodies; the huge bird in the center waiting to be cut. Ron performs the complicated operation under the crowd's admiring eyes.

We help ourselves to the delicious turkey and all the accompanying goodies, including my Mideastern contribution.

Mark relates to Dea and me the history of the Indian-American Thanksgiving.

"Aren't we hypocrites?" he asks.

I shrug.

"Well, at least you remember their hospitality once a year," says Dea.

Mark filled her plate and is watching over her. The moment her glass is empty he rushes to refill it, he is attentive to her and his face lightens up whenever she talks. She seems very happy and there is a glow around them, the in-love glow that separates them from the rest of the world.

I don't want to pester you, wherever you are, but I don't remember you being as attentive to me, not during our first days, weeks, years. There was a kind of condescending humor, sometimes patronizing, and I always thought it was because I was younger, but you never treated Dea that way. I should not complain: it is with this very behavior of yours I fell in love; I loved the way I seemed to amuse you no matter what I did or say. Like a child entertaining an adult. In a way it was as if you didn't take me too seriously.

"What are you brooding about?" asks Dea.

I want to say, *Nothing*, but by the way she looks at me I know she knows I am thinking about you. So she just caresses my arm and both she and Mark raise their glasses.

"To you and to your future happiness," says Dea.

"May I join in?" asks Ron.

"By all means," says Dea.

Ron raises his glass and declares, "I will drink to being happy here and now," and he looks me in the eyes. I feel my cheeks are burning. Is it early menopause or old embarrassment?

I wonder, as I often do about new acquaintances, *Does he know?* I guess he doesn't, and as much as I am obsessed with Alon's death, it is not written on my face. Maybe I should wear black constantly and never go out. But they don't leave me to my gloomy thoughts. Mark is refilling my glass and my plate as well, Ron is entertaining me with funny anecdotes, Dea is looking at me with new warmth in her eyes and Karen makes sure I am introduced and that I chat with every guest of hers.

I feel warm, and maybe it is the fireplace burning gaily, but I think it's the hospitality, the welcoming people, their acceptance, their friendliness and warmth. I don't feel like a stranger in Karen's house on Thanksgiving and I am thankful.

WINTER

I woke up this morning to my first snow at the barn. It was even more beautiful than I anticipated. Everything in sight wears a white cloak, the meadow, the cornfield, the trees. The snow is falling soft and silent, and it is all illuminated as if there was a full moon shining down. I feel more cutout than ever, all alone in this silent, virginal, isolated wilderness.

I put on some warm clothes and a pair of boots and take astonished Rita out to her first snow ever. She stands puzzled by this new sight, sound, feel, view, smell, and then starts exploring the white shimmering miracle, she breathes it, eats it, drinks it, plays with it, sits in it, sprawls on it, enjoying the smoothness and the coldness. Her rich fur is needed today and we both are intoxicated with fresh, pristine air.

Despite promises made in summertime, no one has cleared the snow that's deep on my road. I venture out with my four wheels and good will. The car slides slightly but mounts the snow with confidence I do not have. I drive slowly up my fluff-covered road, looking with awe at the branches heavy with snow, the color of the pallid ground.

I get safely to the highway and drive on a snow-free road all the way to college. I can see some cars stuck in the snow and one accident, but no one stops to stare.

The end of the semester is in sight but I still have things I want to do in class. I am looking forward to today's class, since I intend to talk about the participation and curiosity essay.

Last time I showed my class an abridged video version of Ibsen's *Doll's House* and two of my brilliant students felt that by watching it they were sort of intruding into the Helmers' private lives. *We are like voyeurs,* they complained. I tried to tell them that that is what art is all about. Remembering Ron's Thanksgiving's advice, I gave them an assignment to write down why it is they are so unresponsive in class; they hardly raise their hands, let alone argue. It is not that they are not listening, or that they don't have their own ideas, no, it is just that they do not participate. It seems they lack inquisitiveness and their lack of curiosity is very strange to me, coming from a country where people know and want to know everything about everyone. When there is an accident there are traffic jams mostly on account of the curious drivers.

The assignments I got were enlightening and I intend to elaborate on them in class. Many students described getting up in front of the class as *nerve-racking*, *scary*, *intimidating*. Some women students wrote things like: *I do not consider my opinion to be of much importance*, and many stated, *We are trained to avoid embarrassment*. *I do not allow myself a voice*, admits one student, and many confess to being afraid to sound or appear a *jerk*, *stupid*, *silly*, *dork*, *ignorant*, *nerd*, *inferior*, or *making fools of themselves* in front of *other people*, *who judge us*, or *to be laughed at*. One insightful student wrote: *Oftentimes I look at the expressions of the people in class when asked their opinions on a certain topic and I see a look of puzzlement, almost as if they were waiting to be told what to think*. He goes on to explain that high school was simply that, you were told what to learn in order to pass a test etc. *An argument is seen on this campus as something bad, something we should avoid because it causes conflicts between students or professors*."

Jerry, my philosopher, wrote: *Students are no longer truly students; they have simply learned to be studious. It is a new norm that has developed in America*.

Coming from an argumentative country, where there are so many conflicts, this is a totally new experience, a whole fresh concept, a very different set of norms and beliefs. Strange like the snow, for a desert woman like me, although we do get some snow in Jerusalem, very brief and fast melting.

On the bench across my office building sits a small snow-woman. Or is it? As I come closer I realize it is a young woman, and even closer I recognize Eileen, one of my brightest students.

"Eileen! What are you doing here? You are going to freeze to death!"

All she has on is a pair of jeans and a T-shirt.

"I am fine," she says, hugging herself.

Her lips are light blue.

"Come with me," I order. She gets up reluctantly and we walk to my office. She is shivering. I designate her one of the chairs and go out to prepare her a cup of tea. I put one steaming cup in front of her and warm my hands on the steaming other cup.

I sit and face her. She is avoiding my eyes.

"You missed quite a few classes."

"I know," she says, still avoiding my eyes.

"It is a shame, because you were doing quite well."

Eileen bites her lips, trying to control her tears.

"What is wrong?"

She shrugs. We sit in silence for a while. I take a careful sip of tea. I can feel the warmth spreading in my mouth and down my throat.

"Drink it," I say, pointing to her tea, "it will warm you up."

She holds the cup but doesn't drink.

"My boyfriend is cheating on me," she says at last in a shaky voice.

"I am sorry to hear it," I say and then add, "Are you sure?"

"Positive," she says. "He doesn't even deny it."

"Please tell me more."

"We have been together since senior year in high school. I thought we would be together forever. We spent all our free time with each other. Lately he claimed he is busy, I saw less and less of him. When I asked him he admitted finally he is seeing someone else."

She cries softly, I hand her a tissue.

"Have you been skipping your other courses as well?"

She nods.

"Eileen, you have to go back to your studies. I know you are heartbroken but trust me; time will heal you, even if it doesn't seem that way right now."

She wipes her eyes and nose and sips her tea slowly.

"A famous rabbi said, 'No heart is more whole than a broken heart.'"

Eileen tries to smile unsuccessfully.

"Tell you what; forget the writing assignments you missed. I have an assignment just for you and you don't have to read it in front of the class if you don't want to."

She now looks me in the eyes.

"Write down your story from the very beginning: how you met, how you first fell in love with him, how happy you were and then go on to tell the pain of those last weeks. I think it will help you to see clearer and will make you feel better. But no more skipping classes, okay?"

She nods, not trusting her voice.

"And please," I add, "put on warmer clothes."

"I will," she says, managing half a smile.

"We have to go now," I say, consulting my watch. "It's time."

We walk to the classroom in the snow. I offer my coat to Eileen, but she says she is not cold.

I am surprised to see most of my students have made it to class, but then most of them live on campus so their dormitory is not too far. Eileen is not the only one not dressed for the weather. The students must be used to the cold; one of my students is wearing shorts and a short-sleeved shirt.

I talk to them about participation and curiosity and try to differentiate between curiosity, inquisitiveness, interest, and nosiness, snooping and prying, but it seems as if my students see them all as one. "People should mind their own business," says Aaron. Everyone seems to agree. I get carried away and talk about community awareness, about the world being one global village and that if the US didn't intervene in both World Wars the free world would have been doomed. I refrain from mentioning that I don't feel the same way about the occupation of Iraq.

No one argues, they all listen carefully, but I know that I am the one who has to change and accept the deep-rooted isolationism which is such an important part of the huge island of the USA. It is vast and diverse, and still, an island.

As soon as the class is over I rush to Karen's class. She is still busy talking to some of her students. They all seem more mature and secure, she is teaching upper level courses. She doesn't have time for coffee because she has a doctor's appointment.

We walk together to our cars, the snow softly caressing our faces. I tell Karen Eileen's story without mentioning her name.

Karen smiles bitterly and says, "Oh, I can't even count the number of times I heard such stories from bright students, on some rare occasions even male students! You have a broken heart yourself but you never talk about it."

I am quite taken aback.

"Don't give me that look," says Karen, "you are the one who constantly tells me how direct and blunt you are back in your homeland."

"Right, but you are Pennsylvania Dutch!"

"So I am, but I have an Israeli friend!"

"Indeed you do!"

We are standing next to Karen's red-turned-to-snow-white car. We hug, Karen gets into her car and I walk to my car carefully, trying not to slide on the ice under the snow.

I drive home thinking about Eileen, her broken heart and my broken heart, and telling myself that maybe I should do exactly what I suggested to Eileen, write it all down as a healing process. And I realize I am already in a healing process and have been ever since I arrived here, and I feel lightheaded watching the flurry of snowflakes rushing toward my windshield, making me feel like flying in an unreal, ethereal universe.

*

All senses are red and green. The purse is open, credit cards are being pressed galore, shopping sprees are major tornados, baking scents fill the air, and the sound so very sweet of songs and carols engulfs one and all, yes, Christmas is around the corner and jingle bells are ringing constantly.

No escape. I know; we mourners are party spoilers. We cannot celebrate keeping in mind the bygone dear ones who were here just a moment ago, maybe last Christmas. Christmas is not our time of year, and yet I was invited to the faculty Christmas party and I am going. I didn't intend to go but Karen talked me into it, and I even have an old dress you never liked—not my style, you insisted. If sexy was on my list that's how I would have described the dress, but sex is not on my list—did I hear someone say, "Yet?" Is it you, my wanting ghost? The dress is fluffy and suggestive and nothing like I ever dared wear when you were around. You wouldn't recognize me, Alon. Your shy, withdrawn, humble wifey disguised as an amateur vamp! I am glad you can't utter some snide remarks, although I can guess them beyond your faraway grave.

Why do I sound so aggressive? It beats the apologies that were my way of self-expression with you. You were so overpowering while alive and you still are, an extra-large, king-size ghost. My unrelenting ghost.

Well, I am going to the party and I will do my best to have a ball! By midnight the Merry Widow will turn into a pumpkin or a frog, even if I mix my fairy tales. You did call me Mrs. Malaprop every now and then, most of the time for no real reason. Maybe, just maybe, I neither miss the names you used to call me nor your sense of humor that consisted mainly of making fun of me.

No, I am not bitter, just excited and trying my best not to miss you too much tonight, so that I might have some fun. The party spoiler is you, always watching me, as if there were nothing better for you to do in your under- or upperworld. Sometimes I see you as Mephistopheles rather than the Faust I suspect you were!

You hovered around me when I was grading, commanding me to give B's when I was giving A's and insisting on C's when I was granting B's. I ignored you. I hope I made my students happy the way they made me when I rejoiced reading their final essays.

Oh, but I heard you gloating when I got my evaluation forms! You said nothing about all the encouraging positive feedback, but you were neighing when one of my students wrote, *Teach us something*! It hurt. Karen laughed when I told her. "The nasty one overshadows all nice ones," she said, "it is always the same, for all of us, and no matter how many years we teach."

"I never dare read them," said Patrick, another colleague, "it is too painful." Knowing you, you would have done the same thing; you were never good at accepting criticism. Literary critics who didn't like your books were banned forever from your life. Well, your forever didn't last too long and most of your critics repented after your death and couldn't find enough eulogies to crown the deceased genius, dead prematurely.

Is it your shadow in the mirror? Let me concentrate on my makeup. Too much? Why do you think so? No, it looks fine to me. And it becomes the dress. It feels good to like my reflection, a whole new sensation for me, and tonight you cannot spoil it.

Driving with a dress and dressy shoes feels strange, but I drive carefully the way I always drive here, not being intimidated by crazy drivers like those we have aplenty back home; although our country angers and disappoints me, it is still home.

The ball is being held at the big gym hall, tables have been set, the orchestra playing, and of course balloons, lighting, ribbons—Christmassy red and green.

I have a moment of panic as I walk in, lots of strange faces, happy and smiling, but not at me. I have been teaching the whole semester and I know no one here! But then Karen is coming to my rescue, looks at me and says, "Wow, Daphne, I didn't know you have it!"

"Have what?"

"Gorgeousness!"

"Look who's talking!" and indeed Karen wears a short dress, green and red, revealing a nice pair of legs she usually hides under pants.

"Come and meet Jim, we reserved your seat at our table."

Jim is Karen's new man. They met on the Net a while ago and Karen claims that so far he is a "healing experience." "Oh, don't worry," she says, "time will definitely disclose his shortcomings, but right now he is too right to be true."

And handsome he is as he rises up to shake my hand and smile. "I hear a lot about you and your funny accent!"

"Me? Funny accent?" I say with an exaggerated accent. "I don't have any!"

Karen introduces me to the rest of the company sitting around our table, all of them from our English department, and the only one I know is Patrick.

To my right is sitting the most charming and entertaining man I remember meeting. His name is Scott. An expert on Nabokov. We immediately embark on mutual friends: Pnin, Humbert Humbert, Ada and he has read your study on Nabokov's *Don Quixote* and all your translated books. He says he is a great admirer of yours. He holds my hand in his warm and soft fingers and says, "You cannot imagine how thrilled I was when your late husband was supposed to be our writer in residence! And I can only guess how devastated you are by his death."

He is the first one who refers to your death directly, and I am so moved I can't talk.

"Please forgive me for bringing it up. I was looking forward to talking to you ever since you arrived, but you are never on campus, you teach and disappear! I told Karen I wanted to meet you a long time ago!"

I turn an inquiring stare at Karen, but she is busy flirting with Jim.

"Now, don't be sad tonight," says Scott. "Tonight is a special night since we meet at long last!"

Scott is pouring more wine in my glass and toasts: "To a beautiful woman!"

I assume I blush, since my cheeks are burning.

I am making an effort to eat what Scott puts on my plate, realizing it might help ease the buzz from the wine. He is relating anecdotes I never heard before about Nabokov's life and I am not sure you heard them, no offense.

After dinner dancing is taking place and Scott insists on dancing with me.

"I am a terrible dancer," I protest.

"No way," he says, "I don't believe you."

And he is right, a kind of magic happens. We dance and dance and I am not at all self-conscious the way I always am. I am having fun and Scott is indefatigable. We dance and laugh, tripping now and then on others' feet, drinking wine at our brief recesses and enjoying each other thoroughly.

I don't even stop and think about what is going on, it just seems so natural and enjoyable. Only when the party is about to end do I feel my poor feet.

"It is time to go home," I tell Scott regretfully.

He walks me to my car, the perfect gentleman, tucks me in my seat, looks me in the eyes and says, "I hope this is the beginning of a beautiful friendship. It was a delightful evening."

I drive home blithely, feeling a bliss I haven't felt for many years.

I lie wide awake in my bed thinking about Scott, reliving our evening. I don't feel guilty and Alon is far from my mind. I call Karen in the morning and blurt out, "He is amazing, how come you never mentioned him?"

"Mentioned whom?"

"Scott, of course."

"Oh dear, didn't you realize?"

"Realize what?" I ask impatiently.

"That Scott is gay, sweetie, absolutely one hundred percent gay."

Listening to my silent shock, she adds, "I am sorry, Daphne, I was positive you saw it, it is written all over him!"

*

Pennsylvania's sky is gray today, but glowing. Maybe because it is Christmas Eve. Christmas carols are on the radio all day long and out here it is peaceful. I guess it is still frantic in the mall and downtown, but in the barn it is as quiet as it is going to be everywhere tomorrow, Christmas Day. There is still ice and frost, but under today's rain it is melting slowly and green patches of grass are starting to reappear. So it is going to be only a partially white Christmas, and I am busy preparing Christmas lunch, which is also Hanukkah this year.

I wanted to drive to the airport to meet Dad and Erica, but Amanda said I shouldn't bother, it's on her way and she will bring them over. So yes, I am nervous. Erica makes me nervous. She was not an easy mother-in-law and I felt inadequate in her presence, as if she believed her son deserved someone better, like Amanda, for instance. Alon used to say it is my imagination and that Erica is just cold and undemonstrative toward everybody, but I never felt at ease with her. That she and Dad are traveling together is strange as well, it seems they are spending a lot of time in each other's company.

And there is Amanda. We met only when she came to your funeral. She didn't even stay for the *shiva* because she had to fly back. I was stricken by her beauty and her grief. I didn't expect an ex-wife to be so devastated by the death of a man she dumped so many years ago. Flying all the way to Israel just to attend his funeral!

And as if I don't have enough reasons to get uptight about my guests, there is Benjamin, Diana and Adam, their new baby. At least I have a highchair for him provided by the courtesy of the local Israeli community whose members keep calling me and offering their help time and again. I don't even have Dea to lighten the burden; she and Mark are spending Christmas with Mark's family in Maine.

The doorbell rings, the first guests are here, a good-looking young man standing at the door with your smile—Benjamin! I hug him and go out to help with the baby. Diana seems shy and it helps me overcome my bashfulness. She looks very young and frail. The baby is cute and I can already see some of your features in his not yet formed tiny face. Your eyes, that are Benjamin's as well. I show them around and harvest the usual exclamations. The baby comes into my arms and his fresh scent is more powerful than any perfume. I hug him and a deep, gnawing ache tears me like a sharp dagger. I am holding your grandson, whom you will never see, who will not know you. Diana and Benjamin are too busy admiring the barn and I bury my face in Adam's sweet-smelling plump neck and swallow my tears.

The doorbell rings again and Dad is standing there, older, and tired from his long trip, but I am so happy to see him. I hand Adam to Diana and hug Dad with all my force. I didn't realize how much I missed him. I let go of him and hug Erica, who looks older as well, but not as gaunt and broken as she did when I last saw her.

And only then I see the lovely Amanda. She is lovelier than ever. Tall, magnificent, with a figure of a young woman and a radiant smile. She holds the most beautiful flower arrangement and hands it to me. She hugs me and I feel all of a sudden short and chubby. She stops in her tracks and looks at the barn:

"Oh my, it is more exquisite than I imagined!"

"Come see the inside," I say. But once inside there is lots of commotion while Amanda is hugging Adam, Diana and Benjamin. The baby leans toward her and Amanda is glowing. Erica sees her great-grandson for the first time and takes him in her shaking arms.

I go into the kitchen to make sure my baking duck is not burnt. The duck is fine but I burn my hand, drop a china plate and spill the contents while tossing the salad. So I am nervous, no wonder. For a change you are not here gloating, you have so many dear ones to tend to, your son and grandson and your mom. Not to mention Amanda, your first love. Your only love? I can't even fight with you in my head; you are more absent than usual although more present, you are our common tread, although Erica and Dad look as if they have more ties than family ties. I can see them from the kitchen window on their way to the creek. Actually they are holding hands! My dad and your mom! I knew something was going on, but look at them! They seem in love! Dad is seventy-eight years old and Erica is eighty-one! I know it is never too late for love, but they are related. Okay, by marriage, but still! They have known each other forever! Since before we got married! Back then Mom was still alive and so was your dad. Why am I upset? Am I jealous? Of whom? It is true I was always close to Dad. So? Isn't he entitled to some happiness? Too many emotions and you are not around to make light of them.

Amanda comes into the kitchen to offer help. I know she is about your age, but she looks so young.

"No need, it is all done."

"I don't suppose you get lonely here. It is too magnificent!"

"No. I love it. I wish I could stay here forever."

"I can understand. It is a once in a lifetime kind of house."

"It is precisely what Alon said."

Her face twitches, showing her real age, but then she manages to control it with a smile that irons the old mask instantly.

We both look at Erica and Dad heading back from the river.

"They look good together," she says.

"I didn't know about them. I should have guessed."

"Really? But Dea knows! We joke about it constantly, Eric and Erica, the young couple. I will not be surprised if they plan to elope together, or rather get married in New York City Hall."

I feel a pinch of jealousy again. Amanda and Dea joking constantly.

As if reading my thoughts Amanda says apologetically, "I see her every now and then, she tries to keep in touch with Benjamin."

"Of course," I say, urging myself to act and feel like an adult.

"So how do we go about gifts, you don't have a tree!"

"No," I say, "although there is one outside. I think we shall give them before lunch, what do you think? It is my first Christmas ever."

"Oh right, it is your first! Yes, maybe we should get it over with. How is your teaching coming along?"

"Good. I like teaching here. It is so different from universities in Israel."

"Yes, it is quite different. Do you find time to work on Alon's novel?"

"A novel? I don't know that he was writing one. There is something he was working on for the last several months, but I don't think it was a novel."

"I was under the impression he was more advanced. It occurred to me you would have been able to complete his work if he left enough notes."

"Me? Complete Alon's writing? Oh no, I don't think so."

"It seems you contributed a great deal to his writing. There is no doubt his style improved considerably once you became his editor."

"Thank you. But I don't think I could write any of his books for him."

"You never know," says Amanda, and she smiles. "Maybe you should give it a shot."

"Maybe," I say. I don't think I will ever dare. I didn't touch your unfinished work. It is way too painful. Maybe I will sometime in the future when I'll be able to cope with it.

Dad and Erica are back, and we go about opening the gifts. Dad and Erica brought me an impressive artistic Hanukkah candlestick; Diana and Benjamin give me a pair of earrings Diana made and Amanda presents me with a splendid colorful Indian shawl.

I give Dad and Erica each a pair of warm sleepers, Adam gets his first baby car, Benjamin receives an album I prepared with photos of his father, Diana gets an Israeli amulet and Amanda one of your books overflowing with remarks you wrote on most of the pages.

She looks at the book and opens it carefully and I perceive again a twitch around her mouth as if she is about to cry. She contains herself and hugs me warmly, whispering, "Thanks, Daphne. It means a lot to me."

Amanda helps me sit everybody around the table and with serving lunch. She brought several bottles of French champagne and Benjamin is opening the first.

"Let's toast," says Amanda, "and if you don't mind I will be the first."

We all raise our glasses and Amanda says, "Let's toast to our gracious hostess, to her generous hospitality and to her marvelous abode."

Dad is next, he looks at us all with shining eyes. "To surprising twists in late life's avenues!" and he gives Erica an amorous look.

Erica looks at all of us and says: "To Alon, my son, who brought us all together. May God bless his soul."

I am a bit surprised, since Erica was always known as fanatically antireligious.

Benjamin joins her and says, “To my father, whose absence hurts.”

His wife timidly says, “To all of you a very merry Christmas.”

It is my turn and I am at a loss for words when I hear myself say, “We all loved you, Alon. May you rest in peace and may we find our peace.”

Everyone says, “Amen,” and I am relieved I didn’t say what I really wanted to say: *May you let me find my peace.*

*

By the time we leave dusk is setting, the short winter kind, gone almost as soon as begun. Dea says she doesn’t mind driving at night as long as there are no traffic jams. She has driven all the way from Maine, and complained about the traffic.

I am on my way to NYC to spend New Year’s Eve with Nell and Al. It is the first time I am leaving my beloved barn for more than a few hours. No place can be as beautiful as mine, the surrounding forest, the darkening deer, the noisy geese, the white snow insisting on not melting despite the sun and rain.

At least I left my mansion and dog in good hands; Dad and Erica seemed eager to spend some time on their own in these marvelous surroundings suitable to old-young couples as well as to a sequestered woman. I will not stay long in the city, I have to prepare my spring semester, and anyway, my father and his betrothed are flying back home in a few days. Right now I feel like a kid before summer camp, excited and apprehensive.

Driving by my daughter’s side makes it even more festive and I am looking forward to the quality time in each other’s company tonight and all day tomorrow. We didn’t get to talk much since she had to be with her grandfather and grandmother—now united.

“They look happy together,” says Dea.

“Who does?” I ask, deep in my thoughts.

“Grandma and Grandpa.”

“You knew about them and didn’t tell me!”

“I was positive you knew!”

I refrain from saying something about her discussing it with Amanda.

"No, I didn't realize."

"Maybe you didn't want to."

"Why shouldn't I?"

"Well, it must be peculiar for you, your father having a love affair with Dad's mother."

"I wouldn't call it a love affair."

"No? What would you call it?"

"I don't know. It just seems inappropriate at their age."

"You are so conservative."

"No, I don't think so. It is just strange, don't you think?"

"No, I don't. I think it is romantic and sweet and I wish you overcame your inhibitions and pursued some happiness for yourself."

"I was happy with your father."

"You never seemed too happy to me."

"I was. In my way."

"Mom, all I am saying is that you should go on with your life."

"Dea, I know what you are saying, but it is too early. You know how attached I was, still am, to your father."

"He didn't deserve it."

"I can't believe you are saying this about your dad!"

"I am not saying anything bad about Dad. He was okay as a father. I am referring to him as a husband, as your husband."

"I don't know that I want to discuss it."

"You always avoid any mention of Dad as an inadequate husband. To you."

"What do you mean to me? Do you think he was more adequate for Amanda?"

"Actually I do, but this is beside the point. I don't think he was good for you. Good to you."

"What is the point of discussing it now? He is dead."

"And you are alive! Don't be cross, Mom. What I am trying to say is that it is time for you to move on with your life and not linger on what was mainly in your imagination."

"Why are you doing this?"

"Doing what, Mom? I just don't want to see you as an eternal widow lamenting forever your lost husband because I don't think he deserved it."

"Dea!"

"What? I am driving carefully."

"It's not your driving. You talk as if I didn't know your dad."

"Maybe you didn't. Maybe you idealized him. Maybe you disregarded the way he treated you. Maybe if he didn't die so stupidly you would have split."

"How can you say such horrible things," I blurt out, trying not to cry. "We were going to open a new page, come here and live together in the barn."

"Were you?" she asks in a tone that suggests she knows things I don't.

"Of course! We found the barn together."

"I know you did. Please, Mom, don't cry. I only want you to be happy. To get over him, to live your life. To find real love like Grandma and Grandpa found."

"Maybe when I get to be their age," I manage to say, and we both laugh halfheartedly.

*

Going with Dea on a shopping spree the last day of the year is a special treat. Gone are the days when I was the mom in charge, failing to convince a rebellious teenager that torn jeans and huge tattoos are unbefitting. Now she is running the show, dragging me from one overcrowded store to another, choosing my outfits and making me try on the most daring dresses and audacious shoes.

"I am not going to wear that stuff!"

"Yes, you are, this very night to your party!"

"I am too old for this!"

"No, you are not. You have the body to carry it, look in the mirror!"

There is no arguing with her. She makes me buy outfits I wouldn't have worn even at twenty, let alone as a middle-aged widow. Dea is right; I am conservative, what's wrong with being conservative?

She consents reluctantly to buy a gorgeous dress for herself as well, on the grounds that this is my Christmas gift to her.

It is her turn to stare at her reflection. "It does look good," she consents, "but I wish I didn't have all these refills yesterday evening."

Mark had cooked us a scrumptious dinner, it was indeed one of the best meals I ever had. I am starting to admire him. And as a token of my fondness we spend sometime browsing sophisticated cooking devices till we find an impressive set of utensils to serve his talent, my Christmas gift. Dea says I am getting into the Christmas spirit; that I should keep on the spirit for my party tonight. I tell her that with the outfit she chose for me, everything is possible. She smiles skeptically.

*

New York City is breathtaking on New Year's Eve. There are more lights than usual and Christmas green and red still pervades, even the Empire State Building is colorful and scintillating. The cold gives the city a more lucid and crisp quality, as if an amazing photographer zoomed in and focused on the tiniest detail.

I am on my way to Nell's party dressed in the outrageous dress Dea made me buy and wear, with those horrid, uncomfortable shoes threatening to break down with every step. Dea insisted on rearranging my hair. "I am sick and tired of your hair being pulled back in an old maid bun!" she exclaimed, and now my hair runs wild, falling in waves I didn't know I possessed. Looking at myself in the mirror, I wondered if you would have made a pass at me if you didn't know me. You would. You made passes at most women you encountered.

Big parties leave me cold and embarrassed. I am too shy and not great at socializing. With you around I didn't have to bother, you were the center of any gathering and your charisma kept me in my place, quite invisible. I am not complaining, darling, it suited me fine and you know I would have given everything to have you by my side tonight, regardless of what happened last year and the year before on that very special date.

I get out of the cab at Nell's loft in Greenwich Village. A commercial outdated elevator disposes of me in Nell's gallery, that looks grand tonight. All glitzy, the artwork highlighted, and the huge windows bringing in another masterpiece, the Hudson River ablaze on New Year's Eve.

The large open space is already full of festive, beautiful people. I don't feel embarrassed for a change, probably because my out-of-the way outfit disguises me. Or maybe I don't care. I look alone, but I am not, your immense shadow is constantly hovering by my side. Don't chuckle, darling, you were there even when I mistook Scott for a straight man. I believe he too was in love with you posthumously. A handsome waiter smiles at me. "Champagne?"

"Yes, please."

I stand there glass in hand looking at the green and red lights dancing in the river, when I hear Nell's voice by my side: "Daphne? Gosh, I didn't recognize you!"

"Is it that bad?"

"You look great! Absolutely ravishing! A new you! I am so glad you made it! Come, let me introduce you to some people."

She grabs my arm and leads me flashing her radiant smile at her many guests.

"Here, meet my good friends Nina and Fred Lambert. Nina is one of my artists; you can see her photographs all over the gallery. Nina, Fred, this is Daphne Whitkin, a very talented editor and college professor."

We all shake hands and smile politely. You used to say smiling is an animalistic habit, meaning *I smile therefore I am not going to bite you*.

"Whitkin? Are you related to the writer?"

"I am his wife," I say, "actually, his widow."

"Oh, we were devastated when we heard about his terrible death. I am so sorry," says Nina.

See, even while gone you still are so present.

"We met him several times. He was very special."

I nod my agreement.

"Is this one of your photographs?" I ask Nina, pointing to one hanging next to us.

"It is," says Nina, "do you like it?"

I look at it closely. "Very much," I say. There are two chairs standing side by side but slightly turned away from each other.

"Nina is photographing chairs as symbols of humans, you can almost see the absent sitters in the chairs," explains Nell.

Fred says, "Before chairs she did it with shoes; they too contain missing people." I know you would have made a pun about it, but being used to absences before and since your death, I admire Nina's personification of ordinary objects.

I politely take my leave, another glass of champagne, and stroll in the gallery exploring the rest of Nina's vacant chairs. I look at the well-behaved, well-dressed, well-fed people gathered, talking, laughing, eating, drinking, having a good time. They are so privileged and protected, so lucky to be wrapped with affluence and security, although I know this too can be shattered in a second. I compare them to the people back home, in similar get-togethers, raising their voices, gossiping maliciously, venting their pain and tension, the result of an insecure life and quite a few shattered dreams. As if the American Dream did come true while the Zionist Dream failed to a certain degree. It didn't take into consideration the Middle-East location.

I again find myself staring at the series of huge oil paintings I noticed during my previous visit to the gallery. I stand there looking at the paintings, trying to understand the reason for the deep emotion they stir in me. They are similar, yet different from one another, as if each represents a diverse mood or season of the heart.

"You like them," states Al by my side.

"I love them," I say, "I am trying to understand why."

"Analyzing won't do you good," says Al, "good art should do it to you. Explaining just spoils it."

"You think so?"

"I do. I know you are an analyzer and it is necessary sometimes, but when a painting touches you as deeply—there is really no point."

"No, I suppose you are right. But I wish I could understand why they are so powerful."

"Oh, don't think they do it to everyone. I for one am not so crazy about them, but Nell believes he is the greatest. Maybe because I am jealous," he says and laughs. "May I refill your glass?"

"I shouldn't," I say without conviction.

He takes my empty glass and swims among the throngs of all the well-dressed and quite merry guests, and I am about to turn back to the paintings, wishing to understand their appeal, when I see a big, bear-like, good-looking man standing not too far, smiling at me. I smile automatically and turn back to look at the paintings, not understanding why my heart increases its pounding.

Maybe it is the colors, so vivid, and maybe the composition and maybe my interpretation, a kind of internal landscape, heartfelt scenery full of life and passion, a place I have seen before, a place I will never see again, because life and passion are so remote. Al is right, I shouldn't analyze. He is back by my side with the champagne, my head is spinning but I take a sip from my flute to gain enough courage to turn around and look for the enigmatic man and his suggestive smile.

He is there but his hand rests on the shoulder of a very young and very beautiful woman. It enrages me. I don't know why. After all, there was quite an age difference between Alon and me. He looks at me as if he felt my eyes and thoughts but I quickly avert my eyes and look at Al.

"Sorry?" I ask, realizing he has asked something I didn't hear.

"Would you like to meet the artist?"

"Yes," I say without enthusiasm, afraid it will break the spell.

They are starting their countdown to the New Year and Al excuses himself and goes to find Nell.

I listen to the countdown and remember vividly last year, when I was looking for you frantically, wanting to kiss you at midnight, the moment one year turns into another. Mother used to say that you would be with the person you were with at midnight all year long.

I found you. Exactly at midnight, but you were kissing another woman. Younger than me, obviously far younger than you, perhaps a student of yours, and I just stood there outraged and humiliated, remembering that the previous year was no different and as far as I can recall the year before as well.

Ten

Nine

Eight

Seven

Six

Maybe it is better to be all alone

Five

Four

Three

Two

One. The man looks me in the eyes, raises his glass and mouths with his voluptuous lips, *Happy New Year*. He starts making his way toward me, his eyes in mine, but the young woman by his side puts her arms around him and I turn around and hurry as fast as I can toward the exit, passing by kissing strangers and more kissing strangers, to the elevator, and down to the freezing street full of sound and color, fireworks exploding gaily on the Hudson, and I hurry along the streets as if someone is after me, just to get away from it all. From older men and ever so much younger women and kissing at midnight other women than me. All these cradle-snatchers. Then and now. You and this other man.

*

He is here, touching my new object of joy with respectful and skillful fingers. He closes his eyes and listens to the lingering notes. It sounds magical to me. I look at him apprehensive, waiting for his verdict.

He takes his good time. There is no rush. He pulls another cord and concentrates, tuning to the vibration that trembles under his hands and vibrates in this outstanding space.

"Yes," he mumbles to himself, "that's it, yes!"

"So, what do you think?"

"It is good," he consents at last, "you've got yourself an adequate instrument and now it is finely tuned."

I pay my piano tuner and sit on my new stool before I even hear his car depart. I pass my fingers on the keyboard, smell the slightly old, musty scent. I caress the black and white keys, making love to my new baby grand piano.

I still can't believe this amazing gift that was waiting for me when I got back from New York. Dad and Erica bought it and Dad said, "I don't want to push you, darling, but I always hoped you would go back to playing."

The piano looks as if it were standing here forever. A bit difficult to imagine it with all the animals around in the old barn days, yet the sound is amazing and the first time I sat and tried to play with my rusty fingers I cried. Dad and Erica couldn't see, my back was turned to them. I played from memory, Mozart, Schubert, Brahms, Chopin. Old, beloved friends. I had a whole pile of music sheets they bought or brought with them, I forgot to ask. The acoustics is like in a concert hall. The music resonates and echoes to the ceiling and back, and I am enthralled.

I forgot how good it feels to play. Sure, I can hear my false notes and my off-key blunders, but who cares? I can just imagine one raccoon telling the other: What does she think she is doing? Or one goose to its companion: I wish she stopped!

There is no one to listen and judge except you, my eternal critic, and you—we both know—were the reason I quit playing and gave up this bliss. No, Alon, I don't hear you anymore, all the put-downs: a less than average amateur, an insult to good music, a shameless noisemaker who can't carry a tune. Well, I have no shame anymore and you are not here to hear my playing, and if your ghost is having a difficult time, too bad.

Rita barks. Is this a statement about my playing? Did she perceive a fleeting apparition on its way to hide in the ghost wing? I pay no attention to you or her, so she sits back in peace and listens; she doesn't seem to mind my playing. And actually it sounds fine to me. I am improving, and even Erica, who is to a large degree responsible for your pronounced critical attitude, said she likes my playing. Playing all those melodies gives me great joy. While producing the cascading notes I think about the barn and its surroundings, the meadows and the forest vibrating with the music. The creek may be carrying the music on its little ripples, it is exhilarating!

I am so immersed in playing I forget everything else, I just play and play and my fingers dance as if there were no twenty-five-year break. I was still playing when I was pregnant with Dea, getting farther and farther away from the keyboard. After Dea was born my piano had to find another room, not the baby's room, and next thing you said we should get rid of the white elephant—it was a white piano my parents bought for me when I started playing—and I didn't argue.

I stop only when I can hardly see the notes, the light is fading fast on this wintry day and it is time for me to watch the remains of the sunset.

I lean back in my window seat content and serene; savoring my cadence, still hearing the notes reverberating.

*

I wake up in sweat, my heart pounding fast, trying to hold on to the dream that is about to fade. Maybe it was a bad one. I hear something and this is for real. I freeze and am about to reach for my panic alarm but I can't hear Rita, she would have barked if there was something wrong. I listen carefully, nothing. It could be the crackling of the water in the heating pipes. Still I get out of bed and approach the window. I peek through the shutters. A full moon is shining high in the cold sky. The naked trees are standing tall and meticulously sketched against the luminous sky. Everything is still and calm. I decide to take a courageous tour around the barn.

Rita joins me, wide awake. We explore the empty rooms. I don't dare open the ghost wing. There is a limit to my bravery. I pass by the piano I left open; the ivories gleam in the dark. If I want I could play now, in the middle of the night, who would mind? I play a few notes standing by the piano; the vibrating sounds chase away the last vestiges of fear.

What was I dreaming about? Was Alon part of my dream? If I did dream about him since his death I can't remember. But I feel as if I dreamt about a man. Someone was hugging me. Whispering in my ear. I can't capture the dream, just the sensations. Maybe if I go back to sleep I can re-enter the dream. I cuddle in my down comforter, trying to mellow back to slumber, hoping to capture the dream.

I can't fall back to sleep, my mind is busy with tomorrow's first class of spring semester. I am quite ready, but maybe I should reread my notes. I get out of bed and take the laptop. I crawl back under my comforter and turn the contraption on. I read my notes, trying to memorize them before class tomorrow morning. I am about to turn the computer off, when I see a folder I haven't noticed before. It is called *Faust*. It must be yours. I guess I did see it but was reluctant to check it. Well, this is my gutsy night. I open the folder. There are a series of files. This must be the novel Amanda referred to. How did she know? I open the first file. It is called: *Faust Revived—a working title*. Oh, my darling Alon, you were preparing a surprise for me! You were going to show it to me proud and happy and say: Look what I've got for you!

I start reading.

Your writing is more amazing than ever. I can't stop reading. A whole new world is revealed to me. The writing is so much you and on the other hand something new I can't yet define and I don't even try, too engrossed in the incredible story. You sure were a master of words. But this story has something different. Enthusiasm. Exuberance. Vivacity. And your used-to-be-famous biting sense of humor. Oh, Alon, I fall in love with you all over again. Not that I am over you. Or ever was since I first laid my eyes on you. You are so good with words. And it is a love story! A strange one. Almost beyond death. Is it possible you had a premonition?

Obviously your protagonist is you. A modern Faust getting old and wishing—like the original Faust—to reveal the secrets of life. Only your Faust—who has no name yet—wants a different bargain. He wants to go back to his youth, mainly to his first and only love.

Wait a minute. His old love? Is it what you wanted, Alon? Go back to your youth with Amanda? Why am I doing this to myself; it is only a novel, not an autobiography! But it does sound like a wish list. I have to go on reading but am apprehensive. It is too painful. It reads like a kind of disguised diary. I am treading in forbidden territory. This was not meant for my eyes. I should go on reading and maybe find out, but right now it is becoming too painful. Besides, I have to get some sleep, tomorrow is an important day.

I get up in the morning feeling awful. My head aches, my nose is running, and my throat is on fire. I have a fever but no use checking it, I am starting spring semester today—can spring be far ahead? It seems as if it is far, far away, the exposed trees, the snow turned into ice, the gray, forbearing sky. And the haunting trepidation reading Alon's *Faust* instilled in me.

I have to go; I don't want to disappoint my new class.

I put on several layers; it is freezing out there, the temperature in the teens. Entering my car is like getting into a freezer. One of the few inconveniences of living in a barn: no garage to protect the car and me from the weather. After some congealing moments, the car and its inhabitant warm up and drive carefully toward college. As always, if I make it uphill on my frozen dirt road, I can get safely to the highway. From there it's easier.

I can't get Alon's writing out of my head. I know that I will have to go back home and read it to the end, and then figure out what to do about it. I feel heavy and sad; my presentiment is that something bad and unpleasant is in store for me. But then I suppose I have been through the worst.

*

My first day of spring semester turns out to be better than anticipated. The class is smaller; hence it will be easy to remember every student's name and I'll get to know them faster. To my surprise some of the students I had last semester chose to follow me this semester. Among them is Eileen, who looks lovely and seems to have recuperated from her heartache.

After class I make my way, trying not to skid, to the cafeteria for a cup of tea, hoping to meet Karen. A handsome man hugs me warmly to my utter surprise and when he breaks away I recognize Scott.

"What happened to you?" he inquires.

"I don't feel well," I admit.

"I have the perfect cure for you: a movie!"

"When?"

"As soon as you finish your tea."

"Oh, I can't. I have to go home. My dog is all by herself."

"Come on," he says. "It is no excuse. Is there anything else on your list?"

"I don't know..."

"Come on, let's go! I am buying."

I can't tell him I want to go home and continue reading Alon's new novel. And he does have an irresistible smile. So I am up and on my way to the door when Scott holds my arm. "Pray, Daphne, where are you heading?"

"To the exit."

"We can leave through this one," he says, pointing at the exit next to us.

I look at the door and realize for the first time I have been using only the entrance door to get out. Because of security in Israel there is always only one door open for entering and exiting. Other doors are locked at all times. I stopped preparing my handbag for inspection every time I enter someplace, but this habit takes longer to shake away.

"I haven't been to the movies for ages," I tell Scott while he is driving. The last film I saw was probably with Alon, long before he died. Lately we hardly went out together.

"It is high time you started having some fun!" proclaims Scott.

The film he chooses is a sidesplitting comedy; I laugh wholeheartedly and listen to my laughter amazed.

Such merriment leaves us both famished and Scott takes me to his favorite Italian restaurant, where we engorge ourselves shamelessly with food and lots of wine while he amuses me with stories about his students, his background and his heroic emerging out of the closet. I am having so much fun with my new friend I forget to feel guilty. I feel like a student playing hooky and finally I drive home too full but gay. Alon's *Faust* is in the back of my mind all the time. Still I manage to enjoy myself.

I am driving slowly hearing the frozen ice crack under the wheels of my car, when I see on the driveway to the barn a deer sitting in the middle of the road, hardly budging. I stop the car and wait for her to leave. I haven't yet seen a deer up close before. She looks me in the eyes but stays put. I am looking for the horn, haven't used it since I arrived. In Israel drivers use the horn almost as much as they use the brakes. I blow the horn. She turns her head indifferently. I blow the horn again and only then she gets up and slowly walks away. Before entering the barn I look at her. She is back on the road squatting exhausted waiting resigned for her death. I wish I knew how to help her.

At home I am restless. I want to go on reading your version of *Faust*, but am uneasy. As if something frightening awaits me. I go over my mail, and although I am not sure I have an established credit by now, I am getting lots of credit cards offers. I take Rita out for a brief chilly walk from the basement door, not wanting to frighten the deer. Rita takes long strolls on her own now that she is used to the immobile forest and its hibernating population. With her fur she doesn't seem to mind the cold, my Margarita, another character right out of *Faust*.

I do my daily new exercise: shovel the snow from the path leading to the house, looking at the deer fading into dark, nighttime comes so early and fast now.

I check my email, I play the piano, but there is no getting away, and finally I find myself opening the cursed folder with the many files, mesmerized, reading and reading, completely absorbed by your words, Oh, deceased wizard of telltales, dead wordsmith, departed gifted storyteller, bygone master of imaginative fibbing!

It is your own story. Or rather the fable you wanted to come true. A well-written narrative about a middle-aged man who reviews his life after a heart attack and reconsiders his choices. Everything seems different to him in the light of his impending death. His bleak career and his boring wife, his dreary country, his lackluster life. He wants to trade it all for a new life, a new woman, a new country and a new career, but to appease the gods or the devils, he is willing to settle for less: an old life, wife, country, career. Alon's Faust wants to go back to his past. His past career, his past country, his past wife and his past life.

You did give your Faust a name finally, Michael, and I think I can guess why. Goethe, in his *Faust* refers to a book about ghosts and their incantations written by Nostradamus, whose real name was Michel de Nostredame. But knowing you, you might have intended to pay tribute to Michael Bulgakov, another "Faustian," whose *The Artist and Margarita* you admired.

Yours is an unfinished novel; you wrote about half of it, if not more, the missing part is what happens to Michael when he recovers from his heart attack. Does he really make the change he dreams about? Will I ever find out? Do I want to? I am not even asking if you would have wanted me to.

When did you write it all? You never mentioned it, and you must have been writing for the last year of your life. It is true you had all the time and space you needed and wanted, including a room of your own at home and one at the university.

You used to show me everything you wrote well before it was finished. You consulted me on each step of your work, with each one of your books; after all, I was your editor, or was I fired unbeknownst to me? And how come Amanda knew about this book? Is she Helen? *Was this the face that launched a thousand ships, and burnt the topless towers of Ileum? Sweet Helen, make me immortal with a kiss.*

I rush to the library and grab Marlowe's *Doctor Faustus*. Sure enough it is full of your handwritten remarks. You were fascinated by Faustus' necromancy! I shudder, what am I doing here alone in this isolated house in the middle of a nowhere, in a glacial night, haunted by your spooky spirit, reading tales about transcending death?

Next to the passage where Marlowe describes Dr. Faustus' second contract to sell his soul in exchange of Helen you wrote: *And I will give so much more to be with you my beloved!* Whom did you mean, oh, barer of your for-sale soul!

My heart aches, maybe it is infectious, and your Michael F. transmitted me his heart's disease. I hurt but at the same time anger invades me, I am furious at this man I was married to for so long, this stranger who was willing to discard me like a used pair of socks. Phrases you wrote, presumably about me, flash excruciatingly painful in my mind: *Oblivious to his disgust with her, trusting blindly a love that was never there, pathetic in her futile efforts to please a man who by no means could have been hers.* You didn't give her character a name—degrading, isn't it—but we know who this *daft*, *servile*, *plain-Jane*, *tedious*, and *burdening* wife is. I was accustomed to your snide, malicious, malevolent remarks; I used to attribute them to your short temper, your bad humor, why, I even saw it as a sign of intimacy! Of course it hurt, but I did my best to understand and forgive. That is what love is all about, isn't it? But your manuscript is something else!

And with all the rage and fume engulfing me I can still hear a little crazy voice in me protecting Alon, crying, *It is just a novel, a fiction, a "tale written by an idiot, full of sound and fury, signifying nothing." It is surely not real. It is a mere fantasy born in Alon's fertile imagination. He just used it as a way to vent, to create an unreal world with unreal people who do unreal things. Puppets in the hands of a talented puppeteer, nothing else, like his other fictional books.* So why the conspiracy, the lies, the deceit? He never mentioned the novel, not once.

I am seized by an overwhelming desire to call Amanda at once and ask her. She will have the answers; she knows about the novel, she must be part of the real-life romance. The only thing that stops me is the fear of hearing her say, "I have no idea what you are talking about." I remember all too well the accurate description of the pitiful wife *who was as spontaneous as a rock and as passionate as a stone brick.* Right, I will not call Amanda, I don't have the mettle. But I will eventually. Dea, Dea must have known something as well, she did make a few insinuations. How can a mother call her daughter and ask her such a question? I can't even formulate the question in my mind, let alone ask Dea.

I go to bed and turn and toss around and then get up and take one of those sleeping pills I was given after Alon's death. I sleep heavily and wake up my face wet with tears but a new budding determination to live my life to the fullest, no more the *sorry mistake of a woman Michael wedded in a moment of feeble judgment.*

*

Ice flowers are blooming on the naked trees, catching the light like shimmering glass, glistening and sparkling magnificently frozen. I am trying to concentrate on my students' essays but the beauty dazzles my eyes. I leave my desk guilt-ridden but eager and go out to see what Rita is up to in this freezing although sunny day.

And there stands on all fours my adventurous forest dog, surrounded by some brown stuff and when I get closer I discover the remains of a deer. I hear a scream. Since there is no one else in sight or hearing, it must be mine.

It is probably the dying deer I saw yesterday evening. I noticed the prey birds circling high in the sky but I never would have guessed that my sweet, tamed Rita would do such an unholy thing! And she is not even embarrassed! A dark moustache of fur, not hers, is painted around her muzzle and she seems to carry it proudly!

"Rita!" I hear myself scream again and she immediately drops whatever part she was carrying and comes wagging her tail toward me. I order her back home, trying not to look at all the parts scattered around. What did I expect bringing my city dog out to the wilderness?

I call Manny. He comes at once riding his powerful pickup truck and clears the remains. I keep Rita in and she barks and yelps desperately, craving her carved deer.

"You must be careful with your dog," says Manny. "If they caught her with the deer she could be shot on the spot, people around here are quite protective of their deer."

"Protective? But they hunt their deer, they have enough deer meat for all winter and more!"

"Right," agrees Manny, "but they have a permit. And the hunting season is over."

"I can assure you Rita didn't kill the deer!"

"I know, sure she didn't. But people around here don't stop to think before shooting!"

"Okay, I'll be careful!"

After Manny leaves, I tell Rita, "No more walks on your own."

It hasn't rained nor snowed for a while but the ice and the frost persists, making walks slippery and hazardous. But I will take Rita out whenever necessary.

Back at my desk, I look up Amanda's number and not for the first time today. I reach for the phone, but I can't bring myself to dial. I try rereading some of the more hurtful passages in Alon's unfinished novel so that I can summon the courage to call. But again I find myself succumbing to the writer's undeniable charm and craftsmanship. Yes, I am becoming compulsive. I am looking at some other files and sure enough I find it, an outline. My hand shakes when I click the mouse to open it.

It is indeed a rough outline; just a few points, most of them you treated later in your manuscript. But there are some brief notes about how you intended to go on with your fiction. Yes, the protagonist would have recovered from his heart attack, but, in the writer's words: *The reader should be left with the notion that the narration might have been a fantasy, a dream dreamt by a doomed man on his death bed.* I suspected as much but I don't feel any relief. I wonder if Alon had time to dream a dream while his light turned off so suddenly. Maybe this fable was his last dream before he succumbed to eternal sleep. Will I ever find out?

The phone rings. I look at it with amazement. Could it be Amanda guessing my intentions?

A male's voice asks to talk with Mrs. Alon Whitkin. As if I don't have a name of my own. In Israel they would never call a woman by her husband's first name. The self-confident stranger informs me they—I didn't get who—are organizing an evening in Alon's memory. Passages from his books will be read and a panel be held about his work. He asks if I would be willing to talk about my late husband; after all, I was an expert on his work and his lifelong partner and editor.

"No," I hear myself say, "I don't think so."

He isn't deterred and asks if there is any in-writing project I would agree to submit, and again I say as coolly as I can, "I don't think so." Maybe I inherited some of Alon's nastiness.

He promises to send an invitation and urges me to participate. I don't even write down the date. Let them commemorate without me. And almost absentminded I pick up the phone and dial Amanda's number. I have to find out. The phone rings and rings, but no one answers and I hang up before the answering machine picks up. What kind of message can I leave Amanda?

I return to my students' essays but the back of my mind is editing Alon's novel and I can even think about the content of the missing chapters. Someone crazy in me is rewriting and completing the novel! I try to ignore the voice; I refuse to work on this cursed novel, no matter how good it is. And it isn't: it lacks what all of Alon's work lacks—compassion. He was too self-centered, too occupied with his own being, and there was no place left for real love. Lust aplenty. Every imaginable sin, deadly or other, but no compassion. I must admit that the chapters about the seven deadly sins Michael experiences or imagines are very well written, witty and full of Alon's delightful black humor, but no true kindness, humanity, tenderness, humility or empathy—the stuff great writing is made of.

The phone rings. What now? I pick it up, ready to snap if it is another solicitor of some sort.

"Hello?" I say impatiently.

"Daphne?"

"Amanda!"

"Did you just try calling me?"

"I did."

My heart races.

"How are you?"

"Fine," I say, "and you?"

"Working, working, there is not much else."

"How are Benjamin, Diana and the baby?"

"They are fine. I hardly get to see them."

"Amanda, I found the novel."

She says nothing.

"It is unfinished of course."

"Of course. How is it?" she asks in a hoarse voice.

"Good," I say.

"You don't sound too enthusiastic about it."

"Should I?" I ask without thinking.

"I am sorry," says Amanda. "I didn't realize you didn't know about it until I asked you."

"This is not the kind of fiction he would have shared with me. It is about you two."

"I am sorry," she says again.

"How did you know about it?" I ask.

"He told me. You must realize we spoke from time to time."

"The protagonist wants to go back to his first love," I say.

"It is just fiction, Daphne!"

"Is it?"

She doesn't answer. I listen to her revealing silence. "I think we should meet," she says meekly at last.

I say nothing.

"Would you like to come to the city or would you rather I came to you?"

"I don't know," I say, trying to gain some time. Dreading this meeting regardless of where it will take place.

"Do you need some time to think it over?"

"Yes."

"Fine, I'll call you tomorrow," says Amanda.

We listen to the silence on both sides of the line.

"I am sorry," says Amanda for the third time, her even voice chokes, and she hangs up.

I put the phone down knowing clearly that the novel in writing was not a figment of Alon's imagination. It was a real story, his story, Amanda's story and my sad story as well.

*

Tormented, I wake up far too early after sleeping a few hours. I lie in bed listening to the immense silence, my heart heavy, my eyes stinging, miserable. Unloved, I am unloved; no, dis-loved is more accurate. Like discontinued, like disliked, like discarded. I repeat to myself like a mantra, *I am abandoned, betrayed, cheated.*

Self-pity, I don't indulge in, it is against my education, against my personal non-religion; still the wave engulfs me and doesn't let go.

I force myself to get up and open the shutters. The weather is beautiful: sun shining, warming the frost but not really melting it. It is freezing out, but the barn is balmy and cozy. The wild geese are congregating on the meadow as they have since November. Sometimes they fly around, screaming and screeching, at night as well. The creek is their main attraction. It looks like spring, although the radio predicts some snow storms. But it does give a pre-taste of springtime. Only I don't feel any spring bliss. I feel a frozen hand gripping my chest, squeezing.

Amanda called but I said I wanted to wait awhile and she said she understands. We will have to talk eventually, but I need some time to grasp, to come to terms, to let go of my illusions about my marriage to Alon. And right now I prefer to concentrate on my work and give my best to teaching.

Although I pretend to be busy with the moment, my mind is swarming with memories. I conjure up the past constantly, looking back for signs and signals, any clue that can shed some light on my relationship with Alon. I am going back to our first meetings, seeing the smile open his face when I walk into his classroom, and sitting across the table at the cafeteria, Alon reaching out and touching my hand ever so lightly. I can almost feel our first kiss, there was passion there, he couldn't have faked it! And all the poetic things he said in the beginning! The little notes he wrote me, our long walks on the beach, driving by his side to his lectures, discussing Proust, Freud, Nietzsche and listening together to Mozart. Alon was real and he was there. The joy of Dea's birth! He was overwhelmed standing by my side, wiping my sweat. True, he wasn't by my side all the time, but I felt I could count on him. We used to laugh a lot back then. It is true that with time the distance between us grew, he did become remote, and there were always his wild outbursts out of nowhere, his constant bickering and vicious remarks. It started quite early in our relationship, little insults as if he were testing the waters and when he realized he could get away with it, he became bolder, his comments more acidulous and hurting. My protests were meek and halfhearted, I was afraid to lose him so I put up with more and more malice, telling myself he must be suffering more than I did. Coming to his defense, offense after offense.

I go to the big round mirror in my bedroom. I take off my clothes and stand looking at my loveless body. It is not a bad one. Tall, trim, nice breasts, good proportions. So why then, when it came to sex, Alon claimed I was devoid of life? He used to tell me that in my case he failed as a teacher because he was unsuccessful in turning me into a good lover. Was I really that bad? It is true I didn't think much about sex since Alon's death and even long before, but I can feel the hormones rushing in my blood and I can feel sex is not over for me. But it will take a long time, as long as it will take to sort out our marriage and come to terms with Alon's death.

All of a sudden I remember Nell's phone call after New Year's party. She said one of her guests inquired about me and seemed interested. She wanted to know if she could give him my phone number. No.

I put my clothes on, and go compulsively to the laptop. I open Alon's *Faust* and look for the sex narrations. I read and re-read them.

They are very crude, not at all tender. They do not turn me on. Maybe I am the problem, as Alon used to maintain.

I call Scott. That's when gay friends come in handy. "Scott," I say without preliminaries, "what do you think of my looks?"

"Oh my God," he says, "you don't beat around the bush, do you? Well, now at least I am convinced you *are* an Israeli. Let me think. You are pretty and attractive, if that's what you want to hear."

"No, it is not what I want to hear. I want the truth!"

"Well, the truth. I see. What, pray, has prompted this question today of all days? Has Mr. Right's white horse showed up at the barn?"

"You are trying to gain time to come up with something!"

"Not at all! I think you are very attractive. Can I be blunt?"

"Of course you can, that's what I want: your honest opinion."

"Okay. You dress like an old lady, like a conservative old lady. Your hair is always tied up, you are always buttoned up, you never show a leg and I know you have good legs since we danced together at the faculty party."

"My daughter claims the same thing."

"About your legs?"

"About my style!"

"See? Change your style and all men—straight men—will fall in your lap!"

The doorbell chimes its intricate melody and Rita barks.

"I have to go now," I tell Scott, "someone is at the door."

"Could it be Prince Charming?" he chuckles.

"Talk to you later, and thanks."

"You are welcome, see you soon."

I rush down to the door. A guy in uniform is standing there. "I have the oil delivery," he says.

"Oil? I don't think so. I still have over half a tank."

"Is this the number of your house?" He hands me a piece of paper.

"No," I say, relieved, "it is the farmhouse over there. But no one lives there,"

"I don't know, I was told to fill the tank."

He drives his truck to the farmhouse and I look with astonishment. Could it be? Is it possible somebody is moving to the empty house? I grew accustomed to my solitude; I feel a pang of regret. I don't want neighbors!

I will ask Stella when I take in my rent check next week. She will fill me in on the details. Still, I hope it is a mistake and I will be able to keep my recluse, being a hermit sort of grew on me.

*

It is still freezing cold, but spring is in the air, the sun shines, leisurely melting the snow. Yellow patches of grass reappear. At sunset the naked trees glow, draped in golden-orange veil. The wild geese are lingering, screeching and screaming when they take off in their clumsy flight, frightened by Rita, who takes me for a long walk on her territory through what was the cornfield. It is full of sludge from the melting snow and we are sloshing on, muddy but determined. I try to join Rita on her excursions, especially at night, to avoid deer-sampling temptations. Empty yellowing corn ears are flying around us, lighter than wind as we walk the cornfield turned into a swamp.

I need the walk to take my mind off Alon's novel. My servile self keeps writing, rewriting and editing the book, but only in my head. I haven't touched the manuscript. I never will. Or so I believe right now, still vacillating between anger, fury, despair, sadness and hope. Yes, hope, is it autosuggestion if I tell myself that it is nothing but fiction, and has nothing to do with what Alon felt or planned? I wish I had never read that doomed novel.

On our way back I notice a sports car in the driveway of the farmhouse. Who dared venture into my territory despite the signs posting *No trespassing*? But then I remember Stella's confirmation: indeed, people have rented the farmhouse and will soon move in. I dislike them in advance, what business do they have disrupting my solitude, invading my sanctuary? In several months I have become a hermit, a loner who dreads interruptions! I hope there are only a few neighbors, and I won't be tramped by herds of unwanted strangers.

"I am becoming sociophobic," I tell Rita, who wags her tail. I admit I have been talking to her lately, for lack of someone better. And then she gives a sprint and goes on a wild-goose chase. I stumble behind her, shouting, "Rita!" and fall head over heels into the foul, mushy morass—soft, yes, but cold and unwelcoming. I try to get up but sink deeper. *Don't panic,* I tell myself, panicking and submerging in a wave of self-pity. Rita stands high above me, her head tilted to the side. With a forceful effort I pull myself to my knees and then raise myself up, wobbling slightly, shivering and miserable. I am covered with mud. I walk slowly, squishing, weighed with bog. My clothes are all sullied and dripping, my walking shoes heavy and squeaking. I am treading carefully, watching every step so as not to slide again into the tricky quagmire.

And it is in this outfit that my new neighbors see me for the first time. They are standing on the meadow, not too far away, two men and a young woman. They wave at me eagerly, assuming perhaps that this slimy Frankenstein's attire is my daily habit. I wave my brown hand back at them, spraying muck all over. Rita the traitor rushes gaily to greet the new company, barking and wagging her tail.

"Are you okay?" cries out one of the men.

"Fine," I lie trough clenched teeth. One weighty foot in front of the other, I try to keep some dignity in my heavy trod.

I am embarrassed and humiliated beyond words; I want to hide myself fast. I trudge to the basement entrance and let myself and Rita in with as much grace as one weighing 200 pounds of mud can muster. I go to my mirror and look at the sorry sight and it is so hilarious that I start laughing and laugh till I break into tears that leave some nicely drawn furrows on my soiled cheeks and it is so funny I laugh again. I clean the mess I left on my trail, put all my clothes in the washing machine and take a long, long shower, still laughing and crying alternately.

Later, when I peek out of the window the sports car is gone and so are my new neighbors. I don't think I will ever be able to face them again.

*

It is raining after days of early spring, but even the rain seems part of spring. The pastures are slowly starting to gain their color, vacillating between yellow and green. The temperatures are around 50 degrees, quite pleasant, and some of my students already came to class in summer shorts and short-sleeved T-shirts.

The trees are not green yet, but the moss turns them green before spring's breath. The weeping willow is moss green, foreshadowing the willow in the near future. The sun is playing hide and seek behind the clouds. I can smell spring.

And indeed it is spring break. I invited Karen to lunch at the barn and she arrives promptly with beautiful flowers and a bottle of red wine.

As we eat the hearty mushroom soup I cooked, I tell her about Alon's unfinished novel. I feel strange talking about him to Karen, who never met him. She listens carefully, nodding every now and then.

"So you haven't really talked to Amanda?"

I shake my head.

"You are afraid," she states, "afraid that your worst fears will come true."

I nod.

"In other words, you'd rather go on living in limbo than face the painful reality?"

"I guess so."

Karen takes a long sip of her wine and says: "Don't be mad at me, Daphne, but my hunch is that you have been living that way for a very long time. Long before Alon died."

"Tell me something I don't know."

"Why?" she asks.

I shrug.

"Come on," she says, "you must know."

"No, honest I don't. I think about it constantly."

"Maybe, just maybe, you don't want to face the fact that your marriage was not all you wanted it to be."

I nod.

"Was Alon the first man in your life?"

"You sure don't behave like your average shy never-ask-embarrassing-questions Pennsylvania Dutch."

"Well, don't forget I had some years in Sin City."

"Right. No, Alon was not my first man. I had another man before him and he broke my heart into tiny pieces."

"Could it be a pattern?"

"Yes," I say very quietly, "it is presumably a pattern, but you know better than anybody else how difficult it is to break away."

"I know," she says, "and I did break mine. No man will ever brutalize me."

"I'll drink to that," I say, raising my glass.

"I can comprehend why you wanted to live in a make-believe world in the past, I know, I have been there as well. However, what I can't understand is why you insist on distorting the present as well. It is all we have, honey!"

"Detail and elaborate."

"Why do you let Alon be your present, now that he is no longer there for you?"

I shrug. "I wish I knew."

"I have a guess: maybe if you let go of your Alon's fantasy you will have to go out there and replace him with someone real. Someone who will reciprocate your love. One-sided love is doomed, Daphne, I have been there. It is not the way things are meant to be. You can't go on loving a man who doesn't love you back, even if he is dead!"

These are harsh words and I am at a loss for an answer.

"Let me show you something," says Karen, getting up from her seat. "Where is your computer?"

"Upstairs."

"So let's go."

I follow Karen. She sits in front of the computer, motioning to a chair nearby.

She types an address and then clicks into a site I have never seen before.

"Oh no," I say, "you are not going to hook me into one of these."

"Be patient, I just want to show you something," she says while she goes on skillfully filling in some blanks.

"Now watch this," she says.

Rows of photos of different men pop up on the screen.

"Karen, please, I am not interested."

"They don't bite," she says, "I just wanted you to realize there are options. Always!"

"It is too early for me," I whisper.

"Is it, really?" asks Karen, her eyes glued to the screen. "Here," she says, "watch this guy. *Fifty years old, blond, blue eyes, divorced, looking for a career woman willing to go into chapter two*."

"I don't like his face."

"Okay, let's try this one. *A writer is looking for a muse*."

"I had one too many," I say.

"Right," says Karen, and she browses on. "How about this cute one: *willing to relocate for the right woman*."

"I loathe the fact that I have new neighbors, do you think I could stand a man in my barn? How many are there?"

"How many what?"

"Men. On the Internet."

"Thousands and thousands."

"Really?"

"Honey, that's the way to meet people nowadays!"

"It is so…unromantic and pathetic! It is like a market, a love market. They all seem so desperate and love deprived, they were all deceived, misled, rejected, disappointed!"

"They are indeed, but it's better than being alone and ruminating about the past!"

"But I am sure lots of them are just horrible human beings."

"No. Just human beings in search of love, what's wrong with that? I met quite a few before I found Jim. Most were by far nicer than my brutal ex, but there was no chemistry. Like ships passing each other in the dark."

"I didn't know you were a poet."

"Oh, I was one indeed. I wrote lots of poetry in my time."

"And what happened?"

"Life happened," says Karen, "and still I ventured out there and looked for love."

"You are brave, I would never dare."

"You would if you let go of Alon."

"It is too soon," I say. "I need more time."

"Fine," says Karen and exits the site, "I just wanted you to realize that the world is filled with men who can love you the way you deserve to be loved."

"Thanks, pal, you made your point," I say. "Now how about some dessert?"

*

I noticed this morning the leaves are starting to bud on the branches, the colors are changing slowly; spring is about to explode. The deer venture closer to the house grazing happily, still wearing their winter gray. I counted twenty-four deer on my meadow, fawns, older deer, and some moose with their horns white and new like fresh shoots. They grazed, the youngsters played and after a while they flew away, rushing to the forest's haven.

My new neighbors are obviously moving in, trucks and cars come and go, and at nights I no longer have the only light around. I haven't met any of them yet, not considering the mud episode, and if I am lucky it is going to remain that way. Unfortunately Rita differs from me and is already rushing to sniff the newcomers whenever she can.

All of a sudden, out of the blue sky-turned-to gray snow starts dancing and spiraling down, lightly at first and then with vehemence. And in a few minutes everything is white, even the branches. The pine tree next to the entrance assumes again its Christmas appearance. The car is buried under a white cloud. The meadow is re-wearing its white bridal gown. There goes my green! I can't deny the snow delights me all the same; I would love to stay disconnected, today more than any other day.

But the heavy snow lasts for half an hour and stops as abruptly as it began. The sky clears and in a short while the snow melts as if it never was!

And just as the snow evaporates, Amanda arrives at the barn unscathed and looking pale but elegant as always.

I was hoping she wouldn't make it.

I find it difficult to look her in the eyes and I lead her to the living room and without asking make us both some coffee with cognac. It gives me time to compose myself, more or less.

We sit facing each other, the coffeepot between us.

"I know you loved him," she whispers finally.

"Loved?" I ask.

"Love," she says, louder.

"I guess we both did and do. Once this is established, please tell me what was really going on."

"I wish there was an easy way."

"Too late now. Just tell me, is it true?"

"You mean the novel?"

"I mean Alon wanting to get back with you."

"I think so," says Amanda very quietly.

"You are not positive?"

"Is one ever positive? One assumes, guesses, hopes. I thought he wanted to…yes, get back together. I know that's what I wanted for quite a while."

"But you left him!"

"That was many years ago. We both changed."

"Did you make plans together?"

"Daphne, he is dead and so are any plans he might have had."

"I need to know."

"Why?"

"So that I can go on with my life knowing the truth."

"Is there any one defined truth?"

"I know you are a philosopher, Amanda, but in this case there is one truth and I am afraid it is an unpleasant one for me."

"I don't know. Yes, he was toying with the idea, we were, of getting back together, but he was with you and I don't know if he really made up his mind…he did bring you along when he came to sign the contract, to find a house." She looks around and the sore grimace distorts her face.

I get up and go fetch the copy of *Dr. Faustus*. I open it where Alon wrote, *And I will give so much more to be with you, my beloved!* and hand it to her. She reads and rereads and I can see she is straining not to cry.

I try taking a sip of my coffee but my hands are shaking.

"Yes, but he never told you, right? He never said, 'I am going on my own. I want to be with Amanda.' You were the one who chose the…barn with him."

"Are you trying to make me feel better?"

She shakes her head, bites her lips. "No. I assume we will never find out. Maybe it was impossible for him to leave you."

"But he spoke about it with you, didn't he?"

She averts her eyes and says nothing.

"Why? Why did you want him? You had other men while you were still married. You claimed he didn't satisfy you."

"Yes, I did," says Amanda, still avoiding my eyes, "but that was when I was young and attractive and had all the men I wanted at my feet."

"But you are still gorgeous."

She meets my eyes. "Me? Over sixty? Have a closer look, Daphne; you want to see my sagging arms, stomach, breasts? Look closely at my face: two face lifts, I dare not count the collagen and Botox injections I got, trying to fill the gaps, and still the lines tear their way, around my eyes, all around my mouth. Look at my chin, or shall I say chins? More tightening of skin and I'll choke! And I will not tire you with the internal deterioration and the amount of anti-unhelpful medicines I take daily. My body is not a machine meant to last that long. I am old, wrinkled, pathetic. A woman my age is transparent, period, men don't see me anymore. I am past reproduction, past sex, past love. You are too young to understand that."

"But Alon found you attractive. He went on loving you."

"Only because he knew me as a young woman and he didn't see the ravages time inflicted on me. I made sure he wouldn't see them. There is something absurd about an aging Faust craving an old woman." Her face cracks into a cruel mask, revealing her real age. "When he exploded the remains of my illusionary youth exploded," she adds.

"I guess that makes both of us widows." I laugh a short, miserable laugh. Amanda doesn't join me.

"It does make both our children orphans," she says at last.

After a short silence she says, "One never knew with Alon. Did you trust him completely?"

"Yes, I was stupid enough."

"I didn't. And now you don't either and it doesn't make a difference because he is dead and if he were alive he might have left you for me and later me for a younger woman, you know him."

"No, I thought I knew him, but I didn't. Not really. Not because he didn't let me, but because I preferred to live in an illusion and I didn't want to ever wake up."

"You were brave."

"Oh, you were braver if you were willing to give him another chance."

"I always felt guilty, as if I didn't try hard enough our first time around, I mean when we were married."

"So you had a love affair with your ex-husband."

"Daphne, it is all over, he is dead, let's leave him in peace."

"And the novel?"

"I don't know. If it's good it deserves to be published. I would very much like to read it, but it is up to you."

"I don't think I can finish it for him or edit it."

"Of course not. Take your time. Think about it. It is your book now."

"He didn't mean it to be mine."

"Can I keep this one?" asks Amanda, hugging *Dr. Faustus* to her chest.

I nod.

She gets up and sits next to me. She puts her arms around me and we hug each other. And then we both start laughing.

"What?" I say, choking with laughter.

"You tell me."

"If Alon could see us now he would have said..."

We look at each other and cry out laughing, "Kinky!!!"

SPRING

The tree by the living room's window is not sprouting leaves as I thought, but beautiful pink blossoms, spring writing its name in flowers. The weeping willow's thin budding branches are swaying gently in the soft wind, rehearsing their spring ritual dance.

The Canadian geese are still pecking on the grass that gets greener and greener. Grey birds with red-orange vests fly around changing colors like candy. I am consulting books I bought especially, could it be the barn swallow? I read that both, male and female, take turns incubating the eggs! Or is it the red-breasted nuthatch?

I am experiencing again the roller coaster of agony, going through the same symptoms I had after Alon's death, although feeling betrayed is a new shade in the pain rhapsody. It is as if the ache waits for its opportunity and attacks without mercy the moment there is the tiniest crack. I hurt at the least expected moments. And at the expected moments as well: coming back to an empty house, seeing Alon's photo at my bedside, glimpsing the *Faust* files on the laptop, or just waking up at the crack of dawn without remembering what happened.

The pain is different now, it is not the loss of Alon I lament, but the loss of his love, the dis-love I feel, realizing at long last he didn't love me. Or stopped loving me. I feel cheated and rejected, duped, and yes, very dis-loved. Which is a different form of being unloved; this means that if there was love, or an illusion of love, it is discontinued.

I trusted Alon more than I trusted myself. I don't know why. But now, posthumously, I don't. I feel double-crossed, cheated, stabbed in my back, no, right in my stomach. Hurt beyond words.

I have my ways to cope and diminish the distress. I play the piano, I listen to music, I take Rita on long walks, I go to the movies with Karen or Scott and sometimes on my own, a new habit.

My greatest solace is nature. I just gaze out of my many windows and savor the pasture turning greener every day, the budding flowers, the blue sky and the trees striving for their leaves. I take deep breaths of the fresh, balmy spring air and sometimes the grief subsides. At other times the awesomeness of nature is wasted on me, my sorrow and loss are stronger than the elements. And the beauty all around serves to magnify my grief.

Will this roller coaster ride ever end?

Right now I am tense because I have to travel to NYC. Dea talked me into participating in the memorial evening for Alon. She said I had to be there no matter what. She is going, and Amanda called and asked my permission to attend as well. I said yes. I feel our talk has cleared the air, I hold no grudge or barely. It is Alon I blame, not her. Nell and Al will be there too, they all insisted I should be present, no denying I was his reader-editor-consultant, and at least officially still and probably always his widow.

I debated at length about my outfit, and decided against black, although I am cast in the role of the widow. I wear an official blue pantsuit and hope for the best.

I still have lots of misgivings, but I am taking the trip all the same, and decided courageously—or stupidly—to drive there. The organizers of the evening said there is a parking lot I can use, Dea gave me instructions and I consulted some sites for directions.

As I drive up my dirt road I see a car approaching. It is a shining blue four-wheel drive I have seen before and must belong to my new neighbors. I am about to turn aside from the narrow road, but the driver is already reversing his car and goes back all the way up to the main road. I am impressed with this unexpected chivalry and wave and smile as I pass him. He waves and smiles back, but I don't see much of him, just a fleeting sight of a large man behind sunglasses. He does look familiar, but I guess I have seen him before on the meadow when I was incarnating the mud monster, and I did catch several glimpses of him coming and going.

It is a long drive to the city, and I prepared some music to keep me company. I opted for some requiems, appropriate for the occasion. I start with Brahms, my favorite. Spring is gently caressing the trees alongside the road and I have to remind myself to keep my eyes on the highway and not on the splendors nature is spreading profusely on the greening hills around.

The smiling face of my neighbor keeps coming back to me, warm and welcoming, so open. As if we have known each other forever. These are not the expected thoughts of a widow on her way to her late husband's memorial, but I might be doing it on purpose: ever since my heart-to-heart with Amanda I feel alienation I never felt before, and waves of anger and chagrin that come and go.

I should be thinking about my speech but I can't bring myself to Alon's work or place in the literary and social structure of Israel, which is, I believe, the subject of this evening. I will improvise. It is so untypical of me, but then everything since Alon's death is untypical: I can dwell no more in his shadow and be content with being supportive, encouraging and helpful. I have to step forward and make a statement of my own, no more breathing through Alon's lungs, as Dea phrased it. Is this really what I did? I am not sure, I do know he was the center of my universe and that the void he left is immense, but it is filling slowly with my work, my new life in a new country. Precisely what Alon was looking for, excluding me. So there is a poetic justice. What a dreadful, malicious thought! Sometimes I am afraid I inherited some of Alon's unpleasant traits. I feel I am changing, shedding my old skin, growing a new one. I can hardly recognize my new self. Mozart's requiem succeeds Brahms' and I am driving peacefully, with new-gained confidence and contentment. I am learning tranquility and serenity.

My short-lived bliss evaporates when I navigate through the city's labyrinth and get lost, again. I drive regretting, and not for the first time, my unwillingness to have a cell phone. But the beauty of NYC is that I can cross at the next street and indeed at last I manage to find the parking lot.

I am not as apprehensive as I expected to be when I enter the crowded hall. Dea is already there embracing me, as are Mark,

Amanda, Benjamin and people I have never seen before. Alon would have glowed in the admiration. To my surprise I am quite pleased myself. I am promptly installed on the podium, regretting not being able to sit next to Dea.

The evening opens with a young, talented cellist playing Max Bruch's Kol Nidrei, a touching piece of music, and I am having a difficult time not crying, something I have been doing since Alon's death. But now it works, I swallow my tears. I could have had tear intoxication by now.

A professor who knew Alon, and obviously knows his writing well, talks about the impact Alon had on him. He analyzes his contribution and ends by saying how much Alon Whitkin's voice is going to be missed.

The anchorman introduces me, detailing my cooperation with Alon and what he calls my invaluable input to his work. It is my turn to address and I stand up and look around the room. I can see Nell at the end of the hall; with her are Al and a man I know I have seen before, all three smile at me. To my surprise I have no stage fright and I know this is going to be easy.

I start by describing Alon's background. I say it is not really possible to separate the different wars Alon has been through. It was—still is—one prolonged war, far away from its end. I tell them about Alon's childhood in the household of two Holocaust survivors, in the shadow of yet another ongoing war: the war with Israel's neighbors. Alon Whitkin never knew a day of real peace till his life ended as another victim of this never ending war.

I depict life in a country where parents bury their children daily and relate how the abnormal way of life becomes normal and routine both for occupiers and occupied and how occupation corrupts the soul of all sides involved and harbors terror.

I count all the battles in this prevailing war and explain the influence each one had on Alon's writings. I end urging my listeners to never take for granted their relatively sheltered lives and count the blessings of boredom even if it is less inspiring.

There is a moment of silence and then loud applause. I stand there deflated and exhausted, as if I came back from a long trip.

When the evening is over everyone stands in line to hug me: Dea and Mark, Nell and Al, Benjamin and Amanda, who shamelessly wipes her eyes.

*

The neighbors' daffodils are blooming yellow and bright, sparkles of optimism among the chilly remains of winter. It turns out that the branches of the weeping willow are getting greener and greener because the tiny, delicate leaves are starting to form and I can already see them fighting to gain their shape all spiky and eager. It warms my heart. I love spring. I saw in the meadow little blue-violet flowers that look like violets but are actually ivy. Delicate and beautiful. I feel strange, as if spring is transforming me as well. Some new buds are waiting to blossom under my skin, I let my hair loose, wear less layers, and feel lighter.

It is Passover Eve and I am getting ready to celebrate it in the barn, I invited all the guests I could think of. Edna and Ram are visiting and staying with me, Dea and Mark will come later with Nell and Al, and I invited Scott and Karen and warned them that the Haggada we read on Passover Evening has some rather discriminating passages. I asked Dea to prepare Mark as well, I never felt comfortable with some of the anti-non-Jews lines. I invited Lea and Jo, but they are preoccupied with their stressful divorce. Both declined my invitation.

Edna and I have been cooking up a storm yesterday and today, after shopping American style: till we dropped. We decided to prepare the traditional meal with all the additions and our hands are full. Ram is busy peeling and chopping. "We will not have enough food for everybody," I keep repeating like a mantra, and Edna assures me, "We have by far too much."

We set the table for all the many guests; Nell just called to say she is bringing over another mystery guest. So we hasten to add another place on the beautiful oak table that will be fully used for the first time.

By the time I go up to change I am worn out and worried. Hoping this whole enterprise will be successful. Remembering last Passover with Alon and Dad at Erica's—who would have guessed that it would be Alon's last? That I would be here all alone in my amazing barn? That Dad and Erica would be together? They called this morning, evening their time, to wish me a happy Passover. I miss Dad. My first Passover without him.

I put on a long dress, far too dressy, but Edna said everybody would be wearing their best tonight, so I shall too. And although I am tired, I like the woman gazing back at me from the mirror. A smile would have worked wonders but right now I cannot muster one.

The first to arrive are Dea and Mark, bringing flowers, food and wine, but I can't see Nell and Al.

"Where are they?"

"They will be here soon," says Dea, looking mysterious. Sensing immediately my tension, she proposes a little walk down to the creek. I claim the weather is not in favor and neither are my high heels. She turns a deaf ear and I find myself putting on my sneakers and then trying to keep up with her and Rita, rushing to the creek. The creek is churning full of water, the melting snow and the rain contributed to this spring flow so crucial to the growing I can sense all around.

I breathe deeply and try to relax.

We turn to go back to the barn and I see that the neighbors' house is all lit; it seems as if they too are having company.

"Maybe they are celebrating Passover as well," I tell Dea, laughing.

"Have you met them yet?" she inquires.

"Not really. I just saw them from a distance. I don't know who lives there and I don't care. I was better off by myself."

"Oh, Mom, don't be such a sociopath!"

"I am not; I just love my peace and quiet."

"Nobody is going to interfere with your peace and quiet. I am positive he is a very civilized man."

"He?" I ask. "What do you mean by 'he?' I saw several people come and go."

We have reached the barn, Nell and Al are already there, they hug me happily and Nell presents me with a magnificent signed print of one of the paintings I admired at her gallery.

It is so beautiful I want to hang it at once, but I have to introduce my guests. Karen, Scott and Jim arrive, and I am busy taking coats, putting away bottles of wine and making sure everybody feels at home.

I explain that I can't serve snacks or drinks before the *Seder* and Scott says, "Relax, Daphne, we all did our homework; we know what it is all about!"

"I sure hope so," I say and start installing everyone around the table.

"What happened to your friend?" I ask Nell, when I realize we have an empty seat.

"Oh, don't worry, he will be here any moment now."

"You know it is not easy to find the place," I tell Nell.

"Don't you worry, kiddo, for him it is fairly easy." She laughs and exchanges a conspiring look with Dea.

I shrug. "Okay, whatever! You all must be starving so we'd better start."

Everybody is seated and the table looks very festive and although I am still anxious, I look at my guests and feel good. Ram is seated at the head of the table since he is going to lead the ceremony, Edna is by his side. They look radiant.

We are about to begin when the doorbell rings. Everyone looks at me, so I get up and go to the door, followed by barking Rita.

I open the door and see a big man with shining eyes I have seen before, I don't remember where. He smiles, hands me the large bouquet of daffodils he is holding, and says, "The mud lady, I presume?"

I stand there and stare at him.

He laughs, stretches his hand to mine, squeezes it warmly and says, "Hello, neighbor, I have been waiting quite awhile to meet you."

I shake his hand, confused. I have seen him before. "I am Daphne," I say.

"I know. I heard your fascinating lecture at your late husband's memorial. I am Jacque Moralli. Are you going to ask me in, Nell said I could join."

"Oh, I am sorry, of course, please come in."

I stretch my hand to take his coat when I realize he doesn't wear one.

I am trying to understand who this familiar stranger is.

"Do come in," I say, motioning toward the dining room, "we are about to start the *Seder*."

To my surprise he takes my arm lightly as we enter the dining room.

Everyone around the table stares at us as we walk in; I am still holding the lovely daffodils.

"This is Jacque Moralli," Nell addresses the guests. Turning to Jacque, she asks, "What took you so long? We are starving, and the ceremony before food is endless!"

"I apologize," he says while gently leading me to my place, on the other end of the table, close to the kitchen. He sits to my right and smiles.

"So, at long last you meet your unwanted neighbor," giggles Dea.

My neighbor! What a blind fool I was!

"Well we did meet before," says Jacque, smiling mischievously.

"Oh, please don't mention it," I say, and I feel myself blushing.

"Is there anything we should know?" asks Scott.

"We are ready to begin," says Ram, "and before we start I would like everyone around the table to introduce themselves briefly, because not everyone here has met before."

Everyone around the table introduces her-/himself, and I am touched by Mark's introduction: "I am Mark and I am Dea's partner," he says and they exchange a love look.

Jacque looks at me and says, "I am Jacque and I am Daphne's lucky neighbor." And he looks at me with his shining playful eyes. I avoid those blazing eyes but realize all of a sudden where I saw him for the first time: he is the man who raised his glass at Nell's New Year's party.

Ram starts reading the Haggada, and then asks each in their turn to read passages. We alternate between Hebrew and English and follow the traditional ceremony with lots of merriment, not always appropriate to the grave exodus myth told on Passover Eve.

Whenever I look at Jacque he is looking at me with his warm eyes, I can feel his radiating presence by my side and I listen to his deep, soothing voice while he reads his passages slowly and with emphasis.

When the first part is over I start serving dinner. Jacque walks into the kitchen and offers his help, but Dea and Edna are taking charge and we all serve the guests together. I am apprehensive about my chicken soup and sense it's too salty and apologize, but Edna, Dea and Jacque say it is a great chicken soup. I spill some in my embarrassment.

After dinner no one feels like going back to reading the Haggada, so those of us who know a few Passover songs sing them gaily and the rest are trying politely to join in although they obviously are lost. Still I sing aloud with Dea, Ram and Edna and all the consumed wines helps get rid of my shyness. Jacque's presence by my side does not stop me from my singing. When he joins in I ask him how he knows the songs. He says he doesn't, but has been practicing Buddhist chanting.

Before leaving Jacque points at the painting Nell gave me and says: "I hope you really like it."

"Oh, I love it," I say and only then I realize he is the artist.

Alon always complained I was very slow to understand. Probably his way of claiming I am stupid. Right now I feel I am indeed.

*

I saw this morning "my" groundhog running busily around, coming back to life after six months of hibernation. It seems the same size although it went without nourishment for long, cold months.

And yet, winter is still casting its lingering spell. It is cold today like it has been for the last few days, but I guess groundhogs consult the calendar, and the calendar states, *spring is here!* The flowers must know this as well; they ignore the cold and bloom audaciously with the most vivid shining colors, yellow forsythias galore, pink crab apples, lingering white-creamy daffodils. Some daffodils are blooming along the creek. It is a cultivated flower but it spread itself with the help of the wind and the rain. The trees are gradually putting on some color, not green, yet, more like fall colors, as if reversing the process of falling leaves.

The sun is flirting with the weeping willow, endowing the tree with golden green. I am glad the huge tree stands between the barn and the farmhouse and soon will flourish and hide me. I feel as if I am being watched: when I prepare dinner in the wide-windowed kitchen or when I savor my morning coffee at my living room window seat. I know it is most probably in my mind, but I regret my recluse days, when I was the sole inhabitant of my forlorn haven. On the other hand, I can't deny I am curious about the intruder. I even use my binoculars to spy on him. I am very careful not to get caught, of course, but I admit I am intrigued. There is not much I can see, most of the time the farmhouse is deserted, sometimes I see the car drive in, some lights turn on and a shadow cross the window, nothing more. What is he up to?

I take Rita on long walks while I steal glances at the farmhouse, but see no one. Today we venture up the dirt road on our way to the mailbox. I guess the spring affects me: I let my hair down and put some makeup on before leaving, telling myself it will save me time when we come back and I have to drive to college.

Rita is trailing behind me, exploring with great curiosity the different scents and smells that animals and other unseen entities left behind. When I lift my eyes I see my neighbor's blue car driving slowly toward us. I immediately rush back to Rita, take her in my arms and step aside. The car approaches and then stops next to us. I notice my heart increases its beat. I am flushed and upset. The pretty young woman I have seen before is sitting next to Jacque. Jacque gets out of the car and hurries toward me, flashing a big smile.

"Daphne! So good to see you! You look like a spring flower!" he exclaims, and since he can't shake my hands—full of Rita—he plants a light kiss on my cheek.

Rita starts barking at the woman in the car.

"Oh," he says, still smiling, "Dele has her cat with her, that's why she can't make your acquaintance right now. She heard a lot about you."

I look at the young woman, she nods and smiles. I try to calm Rita down. Jacque says something I can't hear.

"Rita, shush," I command, to no avail.

"Would you?"

"Would I what?" I say, raising my voice.

"Join us for lunch?"

"I can't," I say, glad I don't have to lie, "I have a class later."

"How about afterward?" he asks.

Rita is still barking although with less conviction, so I shake my head in a noncommittal way. Jacque gets back in the car, smiles, waves and then drives carefully down the road. I make it to the mailbox on shaking legs furious at myself for feeling so out of sorts and mad at Jacque the cradle-snatcher. Maybe I am able to sense at long last the anger I dared not feel when Alon was alive.

Among the bills and junk mail there is a letter from Dad. I open it up excitedly, relieved to take my mind of older men and younger women.

Darling Daphne,

I wanted you to be the first one to know: Erica and I decided to move in together. It must sound strange to you since we are an old couple. But this is one of the reasons, our days are numbered, we both have been through so many tragedies and we want to enjoy each other's company as much and as long as we have left. We both gave it a lot of thought. We spend most of our time together anyway. I am sure you will be happy for us.

I stand there reading the letter time and again the words refusing to sink. Out of the blue tears are streaming down my cheeks. I am trying to understand why. I should feel glad for Dad. He sure deserves some happiness, but I can't feel anything besides heartache. Why am I hurting? Is it for Alon? For the bliss we could have had? Could we? Or is it that I am jealous? Envy the happiness I will never have? I wish I could feel that way again. Love, being in love, but I had my share. Or did I? I am so confused.

*

I snuggle in bed, refusing to open my eyes, listening to the birds chirp loudly, feigning sleep, ignoring Rita's halfhearted yelps at the door. If I don't open my eyes maybe the day will go away, maybe tomorrow will come sooner, maybe I will not have to go through the next seventeen hours or so, till I'll be able to call it a day. What a day. I wish I could erase it from the calendar, this year and every coming year. A day dedicated to pain and gnawing memories. I wish I could sleep it off, tucked in my enveloping comforter.

But I will go through the motions. Drive to college, teach, maybe work a while in the library, have coffee with Karen, shop for food on my way home. But my mind will not rest and I will be aware of the date every single moment. And there will be the unavoidable phone call to Erica. Long-distance silences and agony ever so vivid. And Dea will call, she will remember. We celebrated with her last year. And what is a year but 365 days and nights, some of them as long as a lifetime?!

Happy birthday, Alon.

Your first one since you died.

I open my eyes, sunshine floods the room. Rain or snow would have been more appropriate, but you are a spring child. Your birthdays were always beautiful. I summon all my willpower and get out of bed. I open the shutters and look at the beauty nature is spreading with such abundance.

Good morning, Rita, do you know today is your beloved master's birthday? Do you remember him at all? I know that if he walked in right now his scent would come back to you at once. But will his scent come back to me?

Rita is hungry and in great need of our morning walk. So we start with the walk. It is colder than it looks. I quicken my steps, almost running, trying to warm up. Down we go to our creek, bursting full of water, streaming with a vengeance.

The most flamboyant red bird is standing on a fresh green branch; that must be the red cardinal, calling out for its mate. Right, mating season is here and everything in sight wakes up with zest. Even I feel more awake than I've felt in a long time.

I turn back to go home where it is warm, a shadow passes in front of the window at the farmhouse. Is someone waving at me? The sun is in my eyes. I don't see a car in their driveway, but maybe they are parked behind the house.

Rita and I have our respective breakfasts, but I have a constant feeling of being watched, so I move to the window seat facing the driveway. The phone rings and I know for sure it must be someone remembering Alon's birthday. I pick up the phone with reluctance.

"Good morning," says an unfamiliar voice, "I just saw you freezing by the creek, would you like some hot chocolate to warm you up?"

I say nothing, too numb.

"Oh, I am sorry. It is Jacque, your neighbor."

"How are you?" I ask politely.

"Fine and warm. So how about the chocolate?"

"I am drinking my coffee and I have to be on my way to college in a while."

"You look like a college student yourself."

College students and cradle-snatching is your forte, I think, but say rather coldly, "Thank you."

"What about later, say dinner?"

Again I am speechless.

"Daphne?"

"Yes. I don't know. It is not a good day."

Why did I say it? So it is Alon's birthday. I hear myself say, "Dinner?"

"Dinner. We can go out or I can cook. Nothing fancy, jeans—like the pair you are wearing now—are great."

"Okay. What time?"

"Whenever you are hungry. Is seven too late?"

"No, it is fine. Shall I prepare something?"

"Build up some appetite."

"I will."

"See you later, I think you know the address," he says, then hangs up, and I peek out the window trying to see him, feeling the panic about to rise. Why did I say yes? It is Alon's birthday! That is precisely why I said yes. And I see in great details last year's birthday. Alon's last birthday. We were in New York and took Dea to a fancy restaurant and they both were so immersed in each other I felt utterly left out. That of course on top of the ongoing flirting with our waitress. But that is not reason enough to have dinner with my neighbor, Jacque the cradle-snatcher. Am I trying to get even with Alon? Ridiculous. I will call and cancel. But then what is the big deal? A dinner with my neighbors, maybe his kid girlfriend will be there, maybe he invited other people. I don't feel like seeing people today. No, I will cancel. On the other hand, it could be fun. Fun? Today? How can I have fun today? Why not? I go on arguing with myself, getting ready to leave the house.

I drive to college but stop the car when I pass by the peach orchard next to the farm at the end of our dirt road. The peaches are blossoming shamelessly. Pink and white. I get out of the car to smell them. Amazing, there were no flowers last time I passed by, when was it, two days ago? They were bare and now all dressed up in blush so lush! I feel light and each blossom inundates me with newly found bliss.

I get back in the car and drive slowly, having a hard time keeping my eyes on the road. The raging spring lures me, displaying its beauties, a cornucopia of wonders. My students are behaving as if summer is here. Lots of bare arms, legs, and lightheaded laughter and excitement. I find it harder to get their attention, so on the spur of the moment I ask each one in turn to recite a love poem. To my surprise there is a buzz in the classroom and every student comes up with the loveliest lines from poems and songs.

Obviously this is their main interest. I should take it into consideration. I don't remember ever seeing the class so animated. I am taken as well, enjoying their verses and their enthusiasm. I manage to forget completely the date until Karen remarks after class, "You look radiant!"

"Me?"

"You!"

"No, I don't think so."

"So why do you blush?"

"No, I don't! Actually, today is Alon's birthday!"

"Well, you don't look it!"

"Karen!"

"Daphne! Is there anything you are not telling me, or yourself?"

"Nothing," I lie to Karen and to myself.

"So let's have some coffee and I will do my best to bring the truth into light."

"I can't."

"Have to go back home to bake a birthday cake?"

"That was nasty."

"Nasty it was and I beg you to forgive my poisonous tongue. I am just extremely curious and was looking forward to our get-together. Besides, I am pissed off and need to talk."

"Okay. Let's have a quick one."

We find a quiet table at the cafeteria, and as soon as we sit down I understand Karen's foul mood.

"I think Jim is unfaithful."

"Detail it and elaborate."

"He disappears. Says he'll call and doesn't. Sounds evasive, and when we are together he is kind of absent."

"It could be a temporary lapse."

"It looks more like a total collapse."

The jumbo sandwich Karen picked up stands untouched on the table. Karen follows my eyes. "Here, you have it." She pushes the plate towards me.

"No, I am not hungry," I lie again. I am starving but promised to build up an appetite.

"You are always ravenous after class," states Karen suspiciously.

"So are you," I point out.

"His line is busy when I call and he doesn't get back to me. When he does he says he is tired and has too much work."

"Maybe he does."

"All of a sudden? And during weekends?"

"Why don't you talk about it?"

"I did. Several times. He dodges off. When I am blunt he complains I don't trust him."

"You don't."

"Should I?"

"I don't know. I trusted Alon and you know how untrustworthy he was. Eat that sandwich!"

"I am not hungry. Well, the upside of this crisis is that I am losing some weight."

"But you don't need to lose any weight!"

"Maybe he finds me unattractive. Too fat."

"Karen!" I cry out too loud and see students turn their heads to look at us. "Look what happened to you!" I whisper now. "The great feminist who teaches young generations about centuries of women's oppression. Who gets upset with the abused women in the shelter where you volunteer because they, as you put it, 'sleep with the enemy,' what has gotten into you?!"

"You are right. But remember where I come from. I was sleeping with the enemy for a long, long time. My wounds are not healed yet; it doesn't take much for me to bleed. For a while I thought I was over my past as an abused woman. That's what Jim did to me. He brought hope and love, passion, romance, trust and happiness into my skeptic, bruised heart."

"He didn't bring anything that was not there. It is all yours, he just allowed you to release it."

"It was hibernating till he came along. And I fear it is about to freeze again."

"You were the one who showed me dozens and dozens of available men on the Internet!"

"Oh, Daphne, they were all frogs. And as Marsha, from the shelter for abused women, says, 'You have to kiss aplenty before one turns into a prince.'"

"So if Jim is acting the way he does he is just another frog whom you turned into a prince for a while. Let him go back to his pond."

"But I care for him. I am involved…"

"Afraid to use the L-word?"

"I guess so. Not right now."

"My hunch is: give him a chance, Karen. One more chance. Let him get over whatever he is going through. And eat your sandwich!"

"Only if you share it with me."

So we both fake, taking tiny bites and having a difficult time swallowing, each for our own reasons, and we smile faint, unconvincing smiles at each other, and then Karen throws away most of the uneaten food and we make our way to our cars.

"I was too busy with my pain to squeeze the secret out of you," says Karen, hugging me goodbye.

"If there will be anything to tell, you will be the first to know," I promise, and I intend to keep the promise.

*

So yes, I go through the motions. The whole array. A long soak in a bubble bath, the choosing of a pair of jeans, shirt, sweater, earrings. The careful application of makeup, and deciding on the best wine in my basement's modest wine cellar. And all the while I go on with the self-defeating monologue entitled *Why Am I Doing This?*

A message from Dad and Erica was waiting for me when I got back home and I didn't call them back under the pretext they must be asleep by now. I heard Erica's grief saying she hopes the day is not too painful for me. How could I respond? No, I am fine; as a matter of fact I am getting ready for dinner with another man.

Am I? Is that what it is? A date on this special date? Will wisecracks take my mind off what I am doing? And what am I doing? Having an innocent meal with a neighbor? Should I have been buried or burned alive after treacherous Alon exploded?

I am getting belligerent, a feeling unknown to me when Alon was still alive. The repressed anger is being released, at long last. Probably too late for Alon to take it, unless he is watching me now. No, I am not vindictive, just getting a new taste for life, and why do I need to apologize for it? To whom?

The days are getting longer and it's still daylight when I cross the short space separating the barn from the farmhouse, hugging the bottle of wine to my heart. I touch the weeping willow's huge trunk for good luck, enjoying its fresh green bursting needles.

"Come on in, it's open!" cries Jacque when I knock hesitantly on the kitchen door, the closest to the barn. As soon as I walk in I am engulfed by a profusion of smells, sweet, spicy, warm, welcoming—hunger overwhelms me.

Jacque stops stirring something bubbling on the stove and rushes toward me, planting a garlic-smelling kiss on my cheek. "I hope you are starving," he exclaims.

I hand him the wine.

"You should not have," he says, smiling. "You look gorgeous," he adds.

"Thanks," I say, "can I help?"

"No, everything is ready."

He leads me to the dining room, a much smaller one than the barn's, but cozier. The style is the same, wooden cupboards in abundance. Fire is dancing gaily in the fireplace, the table is set for two and two candles are already lit. The small but state-of-the-art music system is playing quiet, soft jazz.

"I believe this is your first visit to the farmhouse, right?"

"Correct."

"Would you like a guided tour?"

"By all means."

So Jacque takes me for the grand tour of the house, which is charming, candles burning in the other fireplace, lots of colorful rugs, pillows and comfortable-looking sofas and love seats. The bedroom is simple: a big bed, and one photo on the mantelpiece: a pretty woman smiling warmly at the camera.

"Meet the late Sylvia Moralli," offers Jacque, "a very special wife and mother, I think you would have liked each other." I nod my approval, he sure loved his mom.

Nice paintings are hanging on the walls, but none by Jacque.

"You don't have any of your paintings hanging?"

"No. I need to rest. I have some I am working on in the basement, want to take a look?"

I do, so we go down to the unfinished basement, where there is none of the warmth and order upstairs.

"Sorry for the mess," apologizes Jacque. "I seem to be able to work only in chaos."

Not for the first time I am captivated by his paintings. Even the unfinished ones, and there are several, are amazing. So colorful, so full of inner meanings, so appealing to my eyes. I want to say something but am short for words, too embarrassed. Finally I manage, "It is so, so…"

"It is, isn't it?" Jacque teases me and we both laugh.

"I know you like them," he says after we stop laughing. "You did the first time you saw them, not even knowing who the painter was. I saw you watching them on New Year's Eve. Before you eloped with an invisible partner into the night."

He leads me up to the dining room and installs me in a comfortable chair.

"I hope you don't mind that I already opened some wine," he says, pouring the crimson liquid into my glass.

He sits next to me, quite close. He raises his glass, "To us?"

"To us," I say without flinching, knowing my cheeks are on fire, and not caring. I take a sip, his eyes in mine.

"What a marvelous wine," my new self says confidently, ignoring Alon's voice in the back of my mind inquiring, *Since when did you start knowing your wine?*

"You really like it?" he asks, and he hands me the bottle. I read the label. It says, *Jacque Moralli's vinery.*

"Is it?"

"It is."

"Nell never mentioned this side of you. I had no idea. When do you find the time?"

"Whenever I can go to Sonoma. It is beautiful down there and I am very lucky to indulge in something I love so much."

I take another sip. "It is delicious."

"It is so refreshing to hear you say, 'delicious,' and not 'earthy,' 'mushroomy,' 'raspberry,' etc."

"Oh, but it is all those things!"

"Yes, but you don't use words just trying to impress."

"You don't know me."

"Enough to realize you are shtick-less." He gets up, goes to the kitchen and comes back with our first course: hearts of artichokes stuffed with what looks like meatballs.

"I hope you like it hot and spicy," he says, serving me some steaming hearts.

"I do."

"I figured, you are Mideastern."

"I am," I admit, taking a careful bite. "This is so tasty! It is lamb meat, isn't it? The spices are wonderful!"

"I guess you are really hungry."

"What is the matter with you," I say, surprised again by my new self, "can't you take a compliment?"

"Yes, I can. Thank you, Daphne." He bows politely.

"You are too good to be true," I blurt out, astonished again. It must be the wine, I hardly finished my glass and Jacque is already refilling it.

"I am glad you like my wine and cooking."

"I have a friend who claims all men are frogs till kissed by a princess."

"Oh, but I have," says Jacque softly, "I sure was mighty lucky to be kissed by a princess, otherwise I would have been a frog for eternity."

Nell said he was single so that means a woman he never married. Could it be the Dele kid I saw several times in his company?

"That explains it," I say, taking a mouthful of his savory artichoke. "Well," I continue, having swallowed and enjoyed in silence another tender heart, "at least tell me you are not playing the background music."

"No," he smiles his charming smile, "I don't play as well as you do, although I can fiddle with the fiddle."

"Me? When did you hear me play?"

"Oftentimes! You know the farmhouse is close to the barn."

"You eavesdrop on me!"

"I do not! But I admit I take pleasure in listening to you play especially when you are in the mood to improvise."

"I am not good at improvising," I protest.

"You are too!" he teases and gracefully takes our plates away. I want to get up and help, but Jacque shakes his head and I sit back, sipping more of the rich nectar he produces, impressed and flushed.

"By the way," cries Jacque from the kitchen, "have you noticed a special spice with the lamb?"

"There were several."

Jacque walks into the room carrying an oval dish with a large salmon decorated with dill, capers and rings of lime.

"A special spice in your honor."

"I have no idea."

"Laurel."

"Laurel?"

"Yes. Like Daphne."

"How did you know?"

"I found out that Daphne in Hebrew means Laurel."

"So that is the only reason you used it?"

"Well…" he says and smiles, "the artichoke stuffing called for it, but the salmon—you be the judge."

He fetches another steaming dish, and introduces it: "Pomme Dauphinoise à la Daphne, with laurel."

He serves me generously and I say nothing, so smitten I could melt. It must be the merry fireplace.

I take a taste and close my eyes. "Yummy," I say, "scrumptious." And it is.

Jacque pours his ambrosia into my almost empty glass, I try to protest, but he just smiles his irresistible smile and I give in. I don't know the woman sitting here in my skin, but she is happy and all her defenses are down. Why spoil it?

"So tell me about your work," says Jacque, "do you like teaching?"

"I love it!" I exclaim and relate to him the love lesson I had a few hours ago. Some of the students' verses and lines are still fresh in my mind, and I recite them, encouraged by Jacque's amused smile.

"Wow," he says at last, "I envy your students!"

My cheeks are still ablaze. Why did I have to bore him with my stupid monologue? I take a bite of the salmon.

"It must be cold, shall I warm it up?"

"No, it is so tasty!"

"It must be the laurel."

"Where did you learn to cook?"

And it is Jacque's turn to tell me about his studies in Paris, his love-hate for the French, his beginnings as a sculptor before he turned into a painter. I listen to him, hardly touching the palatial food, sipping his wine, watching his lips move, his eyes glint, enjoying his voice and his words, feeling something deep inside me melt like winter's frost.

All at once he stops talking and looks me in the eyes. I drown in his eyes, soaking in the tenderness of his gaze, wishing time would halt. He reaches over and gently lifts a lock of hair on my forehead. Butterflies are fluttering in my guts. I turn my head away.

"I am sorry," he says.

I turn to look at him. "Sorry? What for?"

He is already up clearing the plates. "I know you are going through a difficult time. You just lost your husband."

"It is almost a year ago," I say, not believing I just said it.

"I know a year is not a long time," he mutters on his way to the kitchen.

I collect several dishes and rush behind him. He is standing facing the barn I left all lit up. I stand by his side. We both look out in silence. I realize he can really see into the barn, my window seat, my desk, the piano, the windows in my bedroom.

"I feel exposed." I giggle nervously.

He turns to face me. He looks sad. "I didn't mean to," he says.

"O no, I didn't mean it that way; I mean that you can see me in the barn."

"Only when the lights are on," he says, obviously relieved.

His warm smile is back, and I just step toward him, caress his cheek and say, "Thank you for a lovely dinner." I am having a difficult time believing I am touching him, yearning for his touch.

"But it is not over; we still have dessert, which I devised especially for you."

I follow him as he puts in the oven two small bowls, each containing, an apple and starts to heat some chocolate bars in a steaming pot. He mixes some spice while stirring the melting chocolate.

What am I doing? I should be out of here. This is wrong. He is a taken man. I can feel his reluctance. I am imposing myself on him. But he insisted I stay. He must think I am a reckless woman. Not even a year since my husband died. He must sense my desperation and loneliness. I didn't know I was desperate and lonely. But I am; how else can I explain this sudden hunger, the craving?

"Maybe I should leave," I say meekly.

He turns to face me. "Daphne, please forgive me for being so pushy. I am just... You are so attractive. I fell for you the first time I saw you on New Year's Eve."

I stand there dumbstruck.

"I am sorry, I will try to restrain myself," he says, turning away, taking some ice cream out of the fridge.

I don't know what to say or do. Part of me just wants to run away and hide, never see Jacque, who has to restrain himself because he is unavailable, and another part in me wants to fall in his embrace and feel those strong arms around me.

So I just look at him completely lost, watching his every movement as he expertly takes the sizzling apples out of the oven and pours over them the ice cream and on top the steaming chocolate.

"Okay. We have to eat it now, when you can still feel the heat and the frost all at once." He carries the bowls back to the dining room;

I follow him and sit down in my place, too numb to smell the aromas of Jacque's creation.

"A last touch," he says and pours some drops on top of his steaming dessert.

"What's that?"

"Calvados." He lets me sniff the open bottle.

"Your making?"

He nods. "Taste," he urges.

I do. I dig my spoon through the hot cold hot cold layers and taste the different flavors. I close my eyes. I open them. I look at him speechless.

"That bad?"

We both burst out laughing and we laugh and laugh, and the laugh is melting my embarrassment and apprehension and when I can breathe again I take another mouthful of his luscious treat.

"Can you guess what is the spice I mixed with the chocolate?"

I am about to say, *No*, but then it hits my pallet and maybe my mind: "Oh my, not laurel again?"

He nods and we laugh again.

*

I am about to call it a long day when the phone rings.

"Daphne?"

"Nell? What happened?"

"It's Al."

I say nothing my heart sinking.

"He had a stroke."

"Where is he?"

"At the hospital. They are going to operate on him tomorrow."

"Would you like me to come over?"

Nell says nothing.

"When and where?" I ask.

She gives me the hospital's address, the time. I can be there without canceling a class but I dare not omit a sigh of relief.

I lie awake and think of Nell. Maybe I should have gone to New York at once. I imagine her lying awake fearing the worst. At least I am not obsessing about Jacque. I try to ignore him since that strange evening, but I feel as if he is constantly there, watching every step I take, although I think he is gone, I don't see his car anymore. I am better off that way, he is too confusing. I still don't understand what came over me during our dinner together.

Poor Nell. I hope Al is going to be okay. They are so happy together. She met him when she was ready to give men up. "My old knight in crumpled armor" she calls him. I should have asked for more details. I will find out tomorrow. Tomorrow will never come. I turn the light on and take a sleeping pill. It has been awhile since I took one; I was quite addicted after Alon's death. And they didn't always help. I just lay awake missing him with every fiber in my body, wishing I could fall asleep and wake up to find it was all a nightmare.

I wake up confused and dehydrated and for a few minutes try to remember where I am. The remains of a strange dream still float in my mind like a torn spider web, but I can't capture it.

Strange noises are coming from the field; I open the shutters and see that the farmers started plowing. The yellowing remains of the corn were already succumbing to the green grass the rain and the sun conceived. The John Deere goes back and forth; soon the earth will be tossed and turned and the rich brown soil will await the seeds to come. Last year, when we came to see the barn for the first time, the furrows were ready to suck in the corn's seeds. Soon the cycle will be completed: four seasons in the barn.

I overslept and I have to hurry to prepare a bag for my trip after class. I leave Rita enough food and regret not having neighbors I can trust, unlike that evasive Jacque, who disappeared all of a sudden. Driving by, I check his driveway: empty again.

The crab apple is blooming along the creek, the willow prospering, almost too green to be true, phosphorescent. It caresses my eyes, all my senses. It must be the color of optimism amidst the pain I have been feeling since Alon's death. The magnolia trees show off their voluptuous flowers, wanton and daring. The pink flowers on the bushes in front of the barn are bursting, singing spring and renewal. It is the season of being born again and again. I feel lighter, each blossom inundates me with newly found bliss.

My students seem quite exhausted, the awakening's spring wasted on them. The end of the semester is close by and they are busy preparing for their final exams. Red eyed, all creased, they can't even enjoy the thought of the nearing summer break. There must be a better way to educate than exams and grading, but I have no idea what it is. One last class, no exams for me, but they have to complete their final essays.

I sit in the bus by the window and take out a book I have been intending to read for a long time. But the book stays closed. Looking at the burgeoning spring lulls me into a kind of bliss and makes me forget the reason for my trip. I will never tire of the beauty of the trees regaining their green leaves, the lavish blooming, the blue sky smiling upon the verdant magnificence.

The hospital's corridors are a study in contrast. They are long and dark, filled with pain and agony. After getting lost for a while in human pain, I find Nell sitting at a small waiting room, gazing into space. She manages a real smile of relief when she sees me. We hug each other silently for a few moments.

"Thanks for coming," is the first thing she says.

"Is he in already?" I ask, motioning toward the operating room.

Nell nods. I sit by her side and hold her hand. We both watch the big clock in front of us, ticking ever so slowly.

"Shall I get you anything? Some coffee? Have you eaten at all?"

"No, just stay with me. It seems forever. The surgeon said it might take some time. It is a complicated operation."

Resting her head on my shoulder, Nell tells me how it all happened. She and Al were getting ready to go out for dinner when all of a sudden he started stammering. Nell thought he was joking the way he often does. But soon enough she realized this was serious. She made him lie down and after a minute or two that seemed forever he felt better. "It is nothing," he claimed, "I had it before; it is nothing but a hunger pang." Nell was astonished but she knew there was no point in arguing. They went out, had dinner, and then she hailed a cab and took Al to the hospital, ignoring his protests. "He is a walking time bomb," said his physician after seeing the tests results.

"His left carotid has a ninety-percent blockage," says Nell, trying to keep her voice steady. "I don't know what will happen to me if the operation fails."

I hug her and say, "He is in good hands."

We sit there for what seems forever. I try not to eye the clock but can't help following the creeping hands hardly moving. I know Nell is watching them too and I am thinking of a way to distract her.

"I had dinner with Jacque," I say at long last.

"Did you?" She turns to face me, something resembling a smile on her face.

"I don't know what to make of him."

"You don't have to make anything. How about enjoying him?"

"Enjoying him? He is so evasive. I can't figure him out."

"He is enchanted by you! He begged me for your phone number for months. I don't think he is evasive or difficult to figure out. You of all people should understand him. He went through his own ordeal, you know."

"No, I don't know. He seems like a playboy to me, a cradle-snatcher, an aging Don Juan."

"Daphne! Not every man is Alon!"

"Alon has nothing to do with it."

"Alon has everything to do with it! You will never trust another man because of him. I told Jacque you were unavailable, that you were still in love with Alon."

"I am not."

Someone in scrubs comes out of the operating room. He approaches Nell and says, "Don't worry, Mrs. Diamond; your husband is doing fine."

"Is he out of danger?" asks Nell.

"We haven't finished yet, but I just wanted to assure you that so far it seems okay," and he hurries back to the operating room.

We both watch the door close behind him silently. I hug Nell, who bites her lips in an effort not to cry. We sit there in silence, and I try not to go back in my mind to the agonizing wait in hospitals while we were looking for Alon and then the waiting at the morgue before dread turned into certainty. Better think of what Nell said about Jacque. Can he really be enchanted by me? Maybe before he got to know me. He sure was disappointed after our dinner in his place. Otherwise how come he disappeared? What was it Nell said about understanding him? I am about to ask her when Nell's friends show up at the waiting room. They hug her, looking worried, and nod at me. They look familiar.

"We met at Nell's new year's party," says the woman, extending her hand. "I am Nina Lambert, and this is my husband, Fred."

"I remember," I say, "I liked your work." And I remember as well they both knew Alon.

"How is he?" asks Fred.

"One of the surgeon assistants came out a while ago and said so far it seems okay."

We all sit around Nell.

"I heard Al made a funny joke about his surgeon," says Fred.

"He did, indeed. The surgeon is Palestinian and Al said that most likely he is the only Jew who paid $10,000 so that a Palestinian could cut his throat," Nell chuckles. "It is so Al!"

We all laugh but then Nina looks at me and says, "I am so sorry, that was rather distasteful."

"No, it is indeed Al's sense of humor. Don't worry about me," I say.

I am bothered, not because of Alon and his Palestinian suicide bomber, but about the racial connotation of the joke. On the other hand, talking about Al's jokes eases Nell's anxiety. That counts right now. And come to think about it, most jokes are racial one way or another.

Now that she has company Nell consents when I offer to bring her some coffee and I feel a mild relief as I get up and walk the corridors for coffee.

Nell is sipping her coffee when the door leading to the operation room opens and out comes a good-looking young man. Nell hands me the half-full cup and walks toward the man, who takes both her hands and says, "He is fine. His carotid is good as new!"

Nell bursts out crying.

"He will be out of the operating room in a moment."

And indeed, two nurses are wheeling out Al's bed. Nell hugs him, still crying. I realize this is my exit cue. I can go back home.

*

Unrest, among all this beauty I feel unrest. Guilty for letting myself indulge in disquiet while all around nature is exposing its marvels. And it was a special day. I should be elated, and I am not. What a shame. I gave my last class today and got the most amazing feedbacks from my students. "I will not forget your course as long as I live," said Matt. "You taught us so much more than literature," said Kelly. And the best moment was when Eileen came to thank me after wining the best essay prize.

So why do I feel so dissatisfied? Could it be the impending trip back to Israel for Alon's memorial? It is true I don't want to go, but I still have time, spring will be gone by then, and I am coming back to my barn, and will teach again next fall. So what is ailing me?

The best remedy will be a long walk with Rita.

It is impossible to stay indifferent to the beauty around the barn. The weeping willow is green and shining, tossing lightly in the wind, the sun illuminating her. The grass turns greener with every sun ray. Next to the creek a tree, a dogwood I believe, is blooming bridal white, flowering her trust in seasons. The raspberries are growing dark green leaves, thorns yet tender.

We go down to the creek; the meadow is dotted with sun-yellow dandelions blooming galore along a blue-violet wildflower hiding in masses in the luminous grass. Bending to smell them, I realize they are not as fragrant as the cultivated ones I used to collect for my mother many years ago. But then the lilacs, blooming in violet-blue and white in tight clusters, smell delicious. Butterflies are fluttering around new as spring. A hiss of cicadas can already be heard rehearsing for summer.

Rita and I check the spring growths. The sun is setting on what used to be the cornfield, turning it to gold. I cut some garlic shoots for my dinner's salad. The creek streams peacefully, a goose screams for its life, alarmed by Rita.

By the time we get back I feel much better, so I sit at my piano and play a Mozart's spring song, singing along in my broken German. I decide to have dinner at my window seat. A colorful butterfly, orange dotted with black, is lying peacefully on my cushion. I dare not disturb it and am trying to work around it, although it might be dead.

A thunder-like earthquake makes me jump up and stare puzzled out of the window: the weather was beautiful a while ago; can it still be thunder? I see nothing so I walk out into the starry night. And then I see it: the magnificent weeping willow just broke down, and is lying there shattered, defeated.

I stand staring at the fallen giant. How could this have happened? Too many new green leaves? Worms eating it from the inside? Why now, at springtime, when everything is thriving? It seems as if the trunk split and fell on the farmhouse. Luckily no one is home. It seems as if there is a dim light in the kitchen, but I can't see clearly, since the tree hides it. I venture among the branches, still vigorous with green life. I hear a faint cry. I rush forward to what was the farmhouse kitchen's door, making my way among the debris.

A great lump covered by fallen branches is lying at the entrance. It is moving and groaning and it makes me freeze with fright. Just when I am about to succumb to my instinct—turn around and run for my life—I hear my name.

"Daphne? Is that you?"

"Oh my God! Jacque!" I rush among the twigs. "What happened to you?" My heart is pounding like crazy. "Are you okay?" I hear myself scream.

He groans.

A large piece of the trunk covers him. *Don't panic,* I tell myself, feeling my nails dig deep into the flesh of my palms.

I start pushing away the broken branches. Jacque lies there muttering things I can't understand and I am praying frantically that he will be okay. Once again I am bargaining in my mind with whoever it is: *Please, please let him survive, let him live,* all the while moving brushwood away, trying to free him.

I can now see his upper body, but not his face.

"Don't worry, we are going to get you out of here," I say, trying to calm him. To calm myself.

"That bloody tree," he gasps.

"We are almost there. Bear with me, sweetheart."

Where did that come from? I hope he didn't hear it. He says nothing so I guess he missed the stupid slip of my tongue. I don't know what comes out of my mouth and no wonder, this whole situation is devastating. What am I doing? I should call an ambulance, the fire department at once; they will do a better job. I might hurt him if I move him. But I go on shoving away branches and trying to push away the trunk under which he is buried.

Jacque is now silent and it scares me even more.

"Jacque? Are you okay? Please talk to me. Jacque! I think I will have to call an ambulance."

"Don't," he says faintly. "Please go on."

So I go on with all my might, moving, discarding; working as fast as possible to release him. I can now see his face distorted and covered with sweat, and it reassures me. Blood is dripping on his face when I bend to have a closer look and I am alarmed but then relieved when I realize my hands are bruised and bleeding.

"Daphne, my savior," says Jacque, and he tries to smile.

"I am not through yet," I say. "Are you in pain?"

"I think I will survive." He grimaces. "My hands are okay, I think." He moves both his arms.

"We should call an ambulance, or at least get Manny to help."

"And spoil our tête-à-tête?"

I presume that since his sense of humor is back maybe his condition is not that bad but when I lift the last branches and manage to push aside the remains of the trunk I see his legs. They look all twisted, his pants are torn and I am afraid to look further. I fall to my knees by his side. He looks at me and smiles faintly. I wipe his brow with my hands, making him look even worse with my blood over his face. It makes me laugh.

"What?"

"I smeared blood over your face."

"Blood?"

"Mine." I show him my bleeding hands. He grabs one of them and kisses it. I stop laughing and allow myself to drown in his eyes. He reaches his hand to my face and caresses my cheek and a moan of pain escapes his lips.

"If you don't want me to call an ambulance you will have to let me take you to the hospital."

"This is too beautiful a moment to waste."

I look at his twisted body. "Jacque, you might have some broken bones."

"Only a broken heart," he says, and he pulls me toward him. I bury my face in his chest and we lie there quietly for a while, but then Jacque tries moving and a groan escapes his mouth.

"That's it, darling; I am taking you to the hospital."

I don't know what is going on, but I am overwhelmed with feelings I didn't know I possessed and I am too scared to think about them.

"Can you get up?"

"Only if you call me darling again."

"Jacque!"

He tries to get up. I look relieved while he moves his right leg and then the left one, but then he emits a cry of pain.

"Can't we just stay here?" he asks in a begging voice.

I lean down and kiss his forehead. I am confused. I can't understand my behavior or my intense feelings. And I am not going to make the effort. Not now.

Jacque hugs me. And I just melt into him on the floor, carefully resting my head on his chest, feeling safe and secure in a way I never knew possible.

We stay that way hardly breathing, but when I raise my head to look at Jacque's face I see that his eyes are closed, and he is immobile.

"Jacque!" I scream, not for the first time tonight. I put my hand on his cold forehead and the other on his heart. He is breathing, his heart is beating, but there is no telling of what damages the falling weeping willow caused. I am behaving like an irresponsible child. I have to call an ambulance at once.

I get slowly to my feet.

"Don't go," begs Jacque his eyes closed, his voice a whisper.

"We have to get you somehow to the hospital."

I take a closer look at his legs and remember the mandatory first-aid course I had during my military service. I need a stick and there are plenty scattered around. I pick one that looks solid and the right size.

"Jacque, where can I find a pair of scissors and a string?"

"The first drawer to the left, beside the sink."

I make my way among the undergrowth and find what I need.

I kneel by Jacque and carefully cut his pants along his left leg. With all the gentleness I can muster I tie his leg to the stick. Jacque moans but I go on.

"Okay, Jacque. Lean on me and let's try to get you up."

He leans on me obediently. We get up very slowly, I see him biting his lips so that no groans will escape.

"I don't know if this is a good idea."

"It is good," he gasps, trying not to lean on me too heavily.

"Here, lean on the wall, I will go fetch my car keys."

"Take mine," he says. "And my purse, we'll need my health insurance."

I am glad he didn't even try to resist, but I hesitate for a second, thinking of the barn's door left unlocked and deciding that Rita will have to chase away prospective thieves merely by barking.

"Would you like a painkiller before we go?"

"You are my painkiller."

We inch our way to his car, I help him sit down. His muffled cries of pain wrench my heart.

I drive the well-known dirt road in the unknown vehicle, trying to concentrate on the road but again bargaining, more like praying in my mind; willing to settle for a few broken bones, but nothing else.

Once we arrive at the hospital I leave Jacque in the car, ignoring his protests, and go in for help. Three paramedics help me move Jacque onto a gurney, and into the emergency room. I fill up the necessary forms at the registration office as if I have known Jacque Moralli forever.

As Jacque lies there and I wait by his side for the physician, I recall my last visit to the hospital in New York just a few days ago.

"I know you were at the hospital with Nell," whispers Jacque, as though reading my thoughts.

"Indeed, I was."

"Complaining about my emotional immaturity."

"I never…" I start saying rather loudly when I see the doctor standing beside us.

"I will have to separate the two of you for a while," says the doctor, "there are some tests we need to run. I promise you I will take good care of your husband."

Jacque gives me his mischievous smile while he is being rolled into the examining room.

I sit on the bench facing the room, and only then realize I am wearing an old, faded sweatshirt all stained from my battle with the willow. Too late to become self-conscious, but I am.

*

It is past midnight when I drive Jacque back home. His left leg is in a cast, he has a pair of crutches, three broken ribs, and he is highly sedated.

"Watch him carefully," the physician said, "he has to rest for a while."

"He will," I said, giving Jacque a challenging glance.

"I don't know what I would have done without you," says Jacque as we turn into our dirt road.

"You would have grown roots and become a weeping willow."

"Stop, Daphne, stop, please stop the car," cries Jacque.

I stop the car, frightened.

"Look at this," says Jacque excitedly. He opens his side of the car and tries to get out, looking up at the sky.

I follow his eyes and then I see it: a rainfall of stars, glittering crossing the sky like a silver ribbon. I hurry to Jacque's side and help him out. We stand there, Jacque leaning on his crutches and me, looking up into the sky, staring at the meteorites' miracle.

"Make a wish," I say.

"My wish has come true," he says, and he turns to face me.

I look into his starry eyes. He limps closer to me, bends his head down and kisses me. My lips open to him, soft and eager. We stand there under the star-dotted sky and kiss as if quenching a terrible thirst.

"Your place or mine?" I ask when the farmhouse and the barn are in sight.

Jacque gives me again his mischievous smile.

"No, no," I laugh, "don't get any ideas. Not the way you are now. You heard the doctor: you have to rest."

"Okay, whatever is more convenient for you, since you are now the nurse."

I look at the big, imposing barn, and at the small, cozy farmhouse. Two big houses inhabited only by two.

"You might feel better at the farmhouse," I say.

"It might be easier for you on your turf," he suggests. "And anyway, I don't care where, as long as you stay by my side."

"I will," I say as I turn into the farmhouse drive.

Getting Jacque in and up to his bedroom is easier this time. I can sense his exhaustion. I help him undress and tuck him into bed. The red message signal by the phone blinks. An opened suitcase lies on the floor, its contents spilled.

"I just arrived," says Jacque, "and haven't unpacked yet. Nell said she might have been wrong about you not caring about me so I rushed home."

"She didn't!"

"No, she didn't. But still I thought..." He extends his hand.

I take it and sit on his bed. "I have to go and see how Rita is doing. I'll get some things and come back."

"Don't be too long," he says.

I bend and kiss his cheek and stand up before succumbing to my instincts and sinking by his side, drowning in his arms.

I go out the kitchen door, amidst the branches still green and alive, yet doomed. Rita barks her discontent. I go up to change into a cleaner outfit. I collect some items I'll need for my sleepover and all the while a small voice in my head asks, *What are you doing?* But I don't bother to answer, I don't know the answer and I don't care, all I want is to be back by Jacque's side. I catch a glimpse of myself in the mirror and look at that new, glowing woman, happy to be in her skin.

My dinner is there, I haven't eaten, but I am not hungry. I toss things back in the fridge, lock the barn's door behind me and hurry back to the farmhouse.

Jacque is fast asleep. I sit on a chair beside him and watch this close stranger I crave. He seems so young with the pain wiped off his face. I want to touch him but dare not wake him. So, little voice, what is it you are trying to tell me? What is wrong with feeling the way I do? His face so vulnerable and touching, my heart goes out to him.

A ringing startles me. Jacque wakes up confused. I hand him the phone wondering who can be calling at this time of the night.

"Hello, Dele. Yes, I was asleep. Yes, I am fine. No, I didn't get your messages. You know what time it is here? I am on the East Coast, remember? Yes, I am okay. No, I was at the hospital. Nothing major. The weeping willow fell. No, don't worry, just my leg. I am in good hands. Daphne is here. She is. So don't worry and quit calling at odd times. I will tell her. Good night, sweetie."

He hands me the phone and I put it back on its blinking base, my hands shaking, my heart sinking.

"Adele says hello," he says. "Why aren't you by my side? Did I sleep for long?"

I sit there dumbfounded, watching him. What does he think he is doing? How dare he talk to Adele while I am here? How can he tell Adele about me? What is wrong with this man, with Alon, with all men? Are they basically and initially polygamous? All of them?

"Lately she is acting more like a mother than a daughter," he apologizes.

A daughter? Adele is Jacque's daughter? How stupid and presumptuous could I have been? A wave of shame washes over me and turns at once to an immense relief.

"O Jacque," I say, getting up from my chair and burying my face in his neck lest he see my stupid expression.

"At least Lenny is busy with his own life."

Lenny. His son. His daughter and his son. So there must be a wife somewhere, and then it hits me, the photo on the mantel is not his mother's. I am stupid beyond belief. I raise my eyes and look at it. How could I have been so blind? Jumping headfirst into conclusions. Right, Nell said he was single, but in English single can mean divorced or widowed as well. And no divorced man would have his ex-wife's photo in his bedroom.

"What's the matter?" asks Jacque as if guessing my turmoil.

"Nothing. Well, just feeling silly."

"You? Silly? You are so bright! Would you mind coming closer?"

I do, and he kisses me again, leaving me speechless, erasing my thoughts. When we catch our breath I take off my clothes and creep into bed, careful not to hurt his leg, his broken ribs.

I lie by his side and hear myself ask, unable to resist: "Jacque? What happened to your wife?"

Very slowly he turns to face me, twitching in pain. "It is a bit like your story, from the little I know. It's strange, people always speak well of the dead, but Sylvia was really special. An amazing wife, companion, mother. And she died the way she lived: trying to save a life."

I move closer to Jacque, my eyes never leave his.

"She was a Buddhist. Not in everything, but she believed we have no right to take another's life. She was always active in different peace movements. Before the kids were born she used to travel back and forth to India, helping the needy, participating in retreats. She was a poet and not only because she wrote and taught poetry, but there was poetry in her way of life."

His voice chokes, I caress his tender face.

"Would you like something to drink?"

"Not right now, thank you, sweetheart."

My heart melts to this sweetheart.

"And then, one beautiful day she was driving on a road pretty much like ours." He smiles a brief smile at me. "We used to live around here, in the woods, surrounded by cornfields. It was dusk, and the deer were out on their evening walk. Sylvia wasn't driving fast, but still there was that deer on the road she saw too late. Too late to avoid her, unless swerving abruptly into the ditch by the road, which she did."

Jacque turns his face from me.

"She broke her neck and died on the spot. She didn't suffer."

I hug him and carefully rest my head on his chest, listening to his heartbeats.

"I guess it was the same for your husband, right? He died at once."

I nod.

"I know you were very close to him. I heard you talk about him at his memorial. Nell said you were very much in love with him. It's not a year yet, right?"

I nod and then raising my eyes to his: "How long has it been?"

"Five years. I know you are still raw and hurting but do you think you can find a tiny place for me in your heart?"

I bend down and kiss his lips. He moans. I draw back, but he hugs me closer, and we kiss and kiss.

"Don't move, darling," I say, "The doctor said you have to rest."

Ever so slowly I caress and explore his aching body, gently licking away his pain, softly kissing his many bruises, getting tenderly acquainted with this new territory, letting passion overcome me, carefully making love to my fragile Jacque, feeling both our bodies pulsate like one.

*

The serenading birds wake us at dawn, and I lie in his arms, blissfully listening to their love song, before opening my eyes to his warm smile.

Morning after morning. Like being in a fairy tale.

"Time to get up," he says.

"The sun is hardly up." I cuddle.

"But we are, and there is a lot to do."

"Oh yeah? Like what?"

"Like work."

Work. We haven't worked much lately. Jacque is still recuperating and I am self-indulging in ways I never guessed possible.

"You really want to work today?" He probably has no idea what date it is. I will say nothing so that he won't feel guilty.

"I do. I have some errands to run. What will you do?"

In other words, he is chasing me away. He wants to be on his own. This is a first and it stings, I wish it didn't.

"I don't know."

"You can meet Karen for coffee, you haven't met since," he hugs me and laughs, "since the end of the semester."

"Now that she is back with Jim she has no time for me."

"Maybe you have no time for her?"

"Maybe," I say, and I hug him with force, his bruises and broken ribs healing.

He kisses me tenderly and the untamed butterflies in my stomach start fluttering their wings wildly, chasing away my doubts and apprehensions.

The sun is already floating high when I get out of bed, hoping Jacque will change his mind.

But he doesn't, and after breakfast I make my way reluctantly to the barn. Anyway, I have to take Rita on her walk and I should start packing, I don't have much time left. Birds of all size and color converge on what's left of the weeping willow. Paying tribute to its dying branches.

Rita tilts her head to the side when we start our walk. Does she miss Jacque as well?

It is a sunny day after some rainy ones. Two pair of geese linger on the lawn, strolling at leisure. All the others flew away; it is too warm for them. They crave the snow and ice up north. The many different forest sounds are back. So are leaves in abundance.

I bend down to greet the flowers who now have names Jacque gave them. There are the gripping summery rose, tulips after April's crocus and narcissus, and the summer's alliums. The lavish flowers in front of the barn and the farmhouse are rhododendron, azaleas, and peony.

I check the cornfield. The corn has sprouted a week or two ago and now is growing taller and greener every day. Rita and I take the long trail today although it is getting hot and very humid. I torment myself with thoughts about Jacque's work and the errands he has to run; I know I shouldn't, but it is a sweet torture, I catch myself smiling just thinking about him, reliving his touch. I like the woman I see in his eyes: bold, sexy and beautiful. A whole new me.

When I get back, Ned, the farmer, is out there with another worker, busy with a noisy contraption that turns the fallen weeping willow into powder. The trunk lies there like a carcass of a prehistoric animal waiting to pass branch by branch through the roaring machine and become green-brown dust. I want to stop them, what are they doing to our willow, but I dare not. Jacque's car is not in the driveway and I feel a pinch of jealousy although I have no idea of who or what.

I go up to the ghost wing and pick up a suitcase. It is dusty and I clean it before standing paralyzed in front of the closet trying to decide which clothes to pack, wishing I didn't have to go. The heat becomes insufferable, and there is no air-conditioning on the second floor. I go down and have a drink of water but what I am really doing is checking on the farmhouse. Jacque sounded so mysterious this morning, what is he busy with? Is he hiding something from me?

Obviously. I can recall now strange phone conversations interrupted when I walked into the room. I have to remind myself that this is Jacque, whom I love. But I loved Alon as well not too long ago and in some part of my heart I always will, in a different way. No, the word I am looking for is not love, but trust. I trust Jacque. I think that he is emotionally mature and therefore responsible. So what is the matter with me? Maybe this happiness is too new and fragile and I am afraid to lose it. Can it be I am still bruised? Is my apprehension part of being so much in love and therefore vulnerable?

This is the moment when women call their women friends to complain and consult. Karen's answering machine is on, and I just leave a brief message hoping she'll call back soon.

I am too restless to do anything around the house, so I decide to use the All-American Remedy and Pastime: Shopping. Now is the perfect time to buy gifts for Dad, Erica, Ram, and Edna. The car is air-conditioned and so is America's Haven: the Mall. By the time I finish shopping the weather has changed completely. Clouds have gathered from nowhere, lightning wounds the sky, thunder strikes and torrential rain pours. As I get into the car, hail as big as little marbles drums on my roof. I drive home carefully, not too worried; somehow Mother Nature frightens me less than plotting humans.

Jacque's car is in his driveway when I get home. I drive to the barn, hoping he will see my car and come over or call.

Nothing. And no message from Karen, as well. Has everyone forgotten me?

I sort out the gifts I bought and slowly start packing, trying to fight the emerging self-pity. Lightning and a severe thunder send me to the window. There is another car in Jacque's driveway. My heart sinks, what is going on? I should call him and find out, but I can't summon my courage, sensing he doesn't want me to.

So that's what is happening to me? I alternated one dependency for another? For so many years I depended on Alon and I now replace him with Jacque? Dependency is a cruel word. But how else can I describe what I feel? And how come I was ready to put up with so much with Alon, but refuse to with Jacque? Do I really? It didn't occur to me before, but yes, I know I will never be able to accept another one-sided relationship. Never again, and I feel relief because I know I am a different woman and not only because I am a happy one, or at least I was till this very morning.

As I go down to watch the sunset I find out the sky has turned innocent blue, everything in sight is green and lush, pearly droplets ornament the bushes and the trees. On the meadow in front of the barn a deer and her fawn graze peacefully, a tiny squirrel is nibbling grass under the window. Sitting in my window seat, I sigh content, no one can spoil that beauty.

And it is in this reflective bliss that Jacque finds me when he rings the doorbell.

"I missed you," he says, taking me in his arms.

"Me too," I mutter into his chest.

"Can I take you to dinner?"

"Can't we stay in tonight?"

"I mean dinner at my place."

"That's different," I say, and we walk hand in hand, he still limping slightly, to the dark farmhouse.

As we enter the living room all the lights turn on and I see lots of people, who start singing "Happy Birthday."

My surprise is complete. Once I regain my senses, I hug Dea and Mark, Adele and Lenny, Nell and Al, who is pale but jolly, Karen, Jim, Scott, they are all here, enjoying my astonishment.

I turn to look at Jacque, the chief conspirator. He smiles his melting smile and says, "Happy birthday, my love."

*

Exhausted and jet-lagged, but staring excitedly out the window, I don't want to miss a thing: not a tree, not a hill, not the green, green grass, celebrating again Pennsylvania's welcoming sky. And welcomed I feel by this season of wonder and profuseness, spring giving in to summer's reign. A year has passed since I last took that same road, from the airport to the barn, but everything is different, I am different.

The endless week in Israel was draining, in painful moments I recalled these splendors and took some solace. The memorial was easier than anticipated, a year is a lifetime. Standing by Alon's grave, I said goodbye to him, something I could not have done a year ago. Explaining to Dad why I chose to come back here was the most difficult moment. Dea helped as much as she could, but he just cannot grasp how a Jew can live outside of Israel. Knowing where he comes from, I understand his feelings.

"Was it painful?" he asks, reading my mind and not for the first time.

I turn to look at him by the wheel, savoring his profile. "Less than I thought it would be. But I felt strange. Like a stranger, a tourist. And I felt a kind of terror I don't remember experiencing before. I went with Edna to the market in Jerusalem and was constantly looking around me, dreading a suicide bomb."

"I worried about you as well."

"Seeing you standing there at the airport, waiting for me, was the best moment of my trip."

"I missed you too. And so did Rita. And a guest we have."

"We do?"

"A wild solitary turkey is roaming our pastures. He must be old and was probably left behind to await his death."

"No, I think he is the first of them. Soon the whole flock will be here. Wait till they start screaming and raise hell at dawn."

"I missed my nature's expert."

"I missed my nature."

"The Great Fireflies Performance, as you call it, is getting better every evening. We will watch it in a while, if you are not too tired."

I am not, I am too exited.

When we finally turn into our dirt road, my heart increases its beats, the sun is about to set, a family of deer stare at us as we pass by. The corn has grown so green and tall the fawns can already find refuge among them.

As the road turns I can see the farmhouse and then the barn. The weeping willow's stump is sprouting fresh, translucent leaves aiming at the sky.

Jacque stops the car, gets out and walks to my side. He opens my door and I get out and into his arms.

I am home.

* * *

Printed in the United States
76505LV00002B/470